'I'm leaving.'

'No, you're not. I won't let you.'

Alix laughed. 'It's too late for the possessive husband bit. You just proved you couldn't care less.'

Rhys drew back. But he said forcefully, 'I mean it. I do care about you: you know that.'

'But you don't love me. You don't even know what love means.'

Dear Reader

Here we are once again at the end of the year... looking forward to Christmas and to the delightful surprises the new year holds. During the festivities, though, make sure you let Mills & Boon help you to enjoy a few precious hours of escape. For, with our latest selection of books, you can meet the men of your dreams and travel to far-away places—without leaving the comfort of your own fireside!

Till next month,

The Editor

Sally Wentworth was born and raised in Hertfordshire, where she still lives, and started writing after attending an evening class course. She is married and has one son. There is always a novel on the bedside table, but she also does craftwork, plays bridge, and is the president of a National Trust group. They go to the ballet and theatre regularly and to open-air concerts in the summer. Sometimes she doesn't know how she finds the time to write!

Recent titles by the same author:

SHADOW PLAY
DUEL IN THE SUN

TO HAVE
AND TO HOLD

BY

SALLY WENTWORTH

MILLS & BOON LIMITED
ETON HOUSE, 18-24 PARADISE ROAD
RICHMOND, SURREY TW9 1SR

*First published in Great Britain 1994
by Mills & Boon Limited*

© Sally Wentworth 1994

*Australian copyright 1994   Philippine copyright 1994
This edition 1994*

ISBN 0 263 78763 X

*Set in Times Roman 10 on 12 pt.
01-9412-52206 C*

Made and printed in Great Britain

CHAPTER ONE

ALIX NORTH had fallen in love with Rhys Stirling the first time she had met him. Her parents had moved to a new house in Kent, to be within easy commuting distance of her father's new job in Canterbury. It was high summer. Alix had gone out to explore the garden, looked through a hole in the hedge, and lost her heart. Rhys had been tall, lean-faced, and good-looking. He still was. But then he had been fourteen and Alix just four years old.

'Hello,' she'd called to him through the gap.

Looking up from the book he was reading, Rhys had spotted her face framed by leaves and came to squat down to her level. 'Hello. What's your name?'

'Alix. What's yours?'

'Rhys. Have you come to live here?'

'Yes.'

'I expect you'll be going to the local school, then—BABS.'

'Babs?' Alix frowned in perplexity.

'It stands for Barkham All Boys' School.'

'But I can't go to a boys' school—I'm a girl.'

'Really?' Rhys leaned closer. 'How can you be a girl with a name like Alix?'

'Well, I am.' Putting her arms through the gap, Alix suddenly launched herself through like a diver, disregarding scratches and torn clothes as she struggled to the other side, then scrambled to her feet in front of

5

him, somehow knowing that it was vital that he should be convinced she wasn't a boy. Rhys, too, had got to his feet and loomed over her, almost as tall as an adult, but she put her hands on her hips and looked up at him with a determined chin as she said in a tone she'd heard her mother use, '*Look*! I am most definitely a girl!'

That had made him laugh. 'Well, you're a tomboy at least,' he'd told her, and taking hold of her hand had led her to meet his mother, who'd given her lemonade and cake. Afterwards Rhys had lifted her on to his shoulders and taken her home, the long way round. Alix had clung on, her arms tight round his neck, and knew herself in heaven.

It had been his turn to meet her mother, but he didn't stay long. When he left Alix ran after him and caught him up in the drive, gazed up at him with a flushed face framed by springy corn-gold curls. 'Please,' she said earnestly, 'will you marry me?'

He laughed again, patted her head, and said of course he would. But he hadn't taken her seriously. He still didn't. But Alix had meant it then and went on meaning it all through the years when the gap in the hedge had been made ever bigger as she pushed her way through, until the two fathers had given in to the inevitable and put in a gate, which saved her mother a lot of mending.

Their two families had become very friendly, all of them diverted by Alix's open adoration of Rhys. He had continued to treat her with good-humoured amusement, playing games with her or letting her come with him when he went walking or fishing in the summer vacations, helping her to learn chess and letting her listen to his music collection in the winter holidays. During term-time Alix didn't see so much of him because he boarded during the week, only coming home for weekends, when he always had loads of studying to do. But when he was free she was a regular visitor, becoming as much at home in his house as her own, and treated almost like the daughter they didn't have by his parents. Alix didn't mind that, but she objected strongly when Rhys treated her like a sister. 'No, you're going to marry me,' she always insisted, supremely confident that he would keep his so-casual promise.

It became a standing joke with their parents, all of whom were confident that she would grow out of it, but was referred to less when Rhys went away to college and then got a job as a civil engineer which sent him to South Africa for a couple of years, and then to build a bridge in Botswana. During those years, when he was home, Rhys was as tolerant of her as ever, enjoying the fuss she made of him and her joy at seeing him. He let Alix go jogging with him every morning and would play a few sets with her at the tennis club from time to time. But a twenty-year-old young man didn't want to be seen by his contemporaries in public with a ten-year-old he'd nicknamed 'urchin'; he met girls of his own age and went around with them, fancied himself in love and gained some useful experience.

When he came home from Botswana he was twenty-eight. His face was tanned now, his features almost as lean, but his body had filled out, become that of a man instead of a boy. He had found strength, not only physical strength but mental self-assurance, too. He had been in charge of an important project and a great many men, and it had given him an authority which showed.

Alix, too, had met a lot of boys and young men, had gone out with some she liked, but there had been no question of any romance; she was just as in love with Rhys as that first day and had no interest in anyone else. When Rhys came home, soon after her eighteenth birthday, she was starry-eyed, convinced that he would immediately be bowled over when he saw her, that they would be officially engaged at once and be married in no time at all. Her mother did her best to dissuade her, but Alix merely laughed and said, 'You'll see.'

When Rhys saw her, grown tall and slender, wearing a very feminine dress and her face made-up, his eyebrows did in fact rise—but he laughed as he said, 'Good grief! It can't be my little Alix all grown-up.'

She gave him a shy, yet breathlessly eager look, expecting him to treat her like an adult, like his girl, but he was only amused, just the same as he'd always been.

He took her out a few times, escorting her to dances, often when their parents came along, too, and Alix was again in seventh heaven, but even she realised that his manner was merely casually affectionate. On the few occasions when she got him alone, Alix tried to tempt him to make love to her. He obliged with a few light kisses, which she found most unsatisfactory. 'Kiss me properly,' she commanded. 'After all, we are going to be married.'

'Married?' Rhys burst into laughter. 'You crazy little idiot! You're not still on about that, are you?' He tweaked her hair. 'You know, urchin, you're really good for my ego.'

Pleased, she said eagerly, 'So when will we get married?'

He kissed the end of her nose. 'Ask me again when you're an adult.'

'I am an adult!'

'OK, when you're not a teenager, then.'

'So when I'm twenty will we get married?'

Rhys glanced at her, laughter in his eyes, but then the laughter died as his gaze lingered on her face, on the long dark lashes and brows that were such a contrast to her fair hair, on her high cheek bones and straight nose that gave her ageless beauty, but mostly on her eyes, as blue as sapphires and full now of loving eagerness. Lifting a finger he traced the tip along the soft, full curve of her lips. 'Maybe I might at that,' he said almost under his breath, so softly that only her alertness let her hear it. But then he spoiled it all by sitting back, giving a twisted smile, and saying, 'You've got a lot of living to do yet, urchin, before you even think of settling down.' A gleam came into his eyes and the grin broadened. 'And so, for that matter, have I.'

Rhys had made such a success of the Botswana project that he was promoted and was centred more on his company's office in London, where he rented a flat. He still went abroad a lot but not for such long periods now, acting more as head of an estimating team for contracts, and also as a kind of trouble-shooter, ready to fly anywhere in the world where he was needed. He was, according to his proud parents, his boss's blue-eyed boy and was heading for a directorship before too long.

As for Alix, she got over her disappointment almost at once, and was happy in the knowledge that in only two years she would be twenty, when Rhys had told her to ask again. And she hugged that murmured 'I might at that' to her like a talisman, knowing that for a moment at least he had looked at her as a woman. She went to college to take a two-year business studies course, refusing to take an additional year that would have given her a higher qualification, because Rhys had said twenty, not twenty-one.

As Rhys was living in London and she was away at college, Alix didn't see him for those two years. His visits home never seemed to coincide with hers, not even at Christmas, because he was away both years and his mother and father flew out to be with him.

By now both sets of parents were the firmest friends; neither had had more children, and they were fast coming to the opinion that Rhys and Alix were absolutely right for each other. Not that they pushed at all; with Alix it wasn't necessary, and Rhys's parents knew that he had a mind of his own. But when the time came for Alix to leave college and get a job, Rhys's father, who had got to know several people in his son's company, found out that there was a vacancy in the London office. She applied and, probably because she wanted the job so badly, survived several interviews to win the position. 'Don't let's tell Rhys. Let's all keep it as a surprise,' his father suggested.

Alix grinned, and kissed him. 'It's our secret, Uncle David.'

Rhys was away in South America when Alix went to work for his company as a secretary. She soon made friends there, her open, animated character making her popular with both sexes. But she wasn't open about knowing Rhys; that she kept to herself. There were a great many unattached men working for the company and several of them asked her for a date—some of the attached ones, too—but she confidently told them that she was already seeing someone and expected to be engaged very soon, so they left her alone.

There was one girl in her office, Kathy, with whom Alix became especially friendly, and who would pass on all the office gossip over lunch. One day they were sitting in the window of a café not far from the office building when Kathy pointed out a girl walking by. 'You see her? That's Donna Temple. She's Todd Weston's personal assistant when he's in London.'

'Todd Weston? He's one of the Canadian directors, isn't he?'

'That's right. And not only a director but the son of George Weston, the company president, who started the firm and still more or less owns it. They say Todd is in the running to inherit the company.'

'And is Donna interested in Todd?' Alix asked, watching the tall, dark-haired girl as she waited to cross the road.

Kathy shook her head. 'He's already married and has a family. No, Donna is putting out her hooks for the man who's next in line to take over from Todd when his father retires and he goes back to Canada.'

'Oh? Who's that?'

'His name is Rhys Stirling, and he is absolutely *gorgeous*. You wait till you see him.'

Alix's stomach turned over and she had to swallow hard before she could say, 'What do you mean—putting out hooks for him?'

'Well, they're a number whenever he's in England— he's away a lot, you see—and everyone's pretty certain that they're having a hot affair.'

'You mean—you mean they're in love?' Alix managed to ask, every word a cut to her heart.

'Oh, no, I'm not saying that. Just that Donna is out to catch him.' Kathy chuckled. 'Although she'll have to be very clever if she does; from what I've heard about Rhys, he has women falling for him wherever he goes. And he hasn't been caught yet.'

That last sentence gave Alix a little comfort, but she said, 'And these women; does he have affairs with all of them?'

Kathy shrugged. 'That I don't know; he's good-looking enough to be able to pick and choose, but he certainly has quite a reputation within the company.' She made a yearning face. 'I just wish he'd ask me.'

'He hasn't, then?'

'Fat chance. Not with Donna around. I mean, just look at her.'

Both girls turned to watch Donna Temple as she walked along the opposite side of the street. In her late twenties, she was rather severely dressed, in a beautifully cut suit that outlined a good figure, walked with head high, aware that she drew admiring glances, and was completely assured and sophisticated.

Alix's heart sank a little—but not very much; she had been in love with Rhys for so long that it had become part of her, but it made her very thoughtful. She had never considered Rhys in the light of other women before; OK, she knew he'd been out with girls, of course she did, but it had never even occurred to her that he might fall in love and marry someone else. She had always been so sure of him. But only now did she realise that there was competition out there. And the competition, in the shape of Donna Temple, might be dangerous.

That was her first reaction. Her second was jealousy. No way did she want to think of Rhys making love to another woman. But there again, she had somehow known that Rhys had become a man of the world, in every sense. But so long as the girls in his life had been shadowy, mythical creatures and could be put down merely to experience, then it hadn't mattered, but it came as quite a shock to see one in the flesh, as it were.

Was Rhys really attracted to that kind of woman? she wondered. Or was he just amusing himself while he waited for her to grow up? Alix decided it just had to be the latter, although she wasn't quite so sure of Rhys as she had been, and she waited with anxious eagerness for him to come home.

From time to time news of him filtered down to her, either at work or at home. From South America he had moved straight on to another project in Australia, so it was over three months later before she heard that he was finally returning to England. The office buzzed with the news, because there was also a rumour going around that old Mr Weston was retiring at last, so there would be a big reshuffle among the directors. A lot of people thought that this was the main reason Rhys was coming home.

Alix heard the rumours but was too concerned with her own reasons for wanting to see Rhys again to think anything else very important. He was due to fly in on a Friday, and everyone, Alix included, thought that he would go straight to his parents' home for the weekend. She could hardly contain her excitement, and had asked for the day off so that she could be waiting for him when he arrived, but a draft contract for a power plant in one of the Gulf states had to be finished and she had to work. Frustrated, and longing for the end of the day, Alix had to sit at her desk and wish the hours away.

But in the afternoon the phone on Kathy's desk rang. She listened then swivelled round towards Alix. 'Hey! Guess what? That was the girl on Reception. She says Rhys Stirling has come here straight from the airport.'

'He has?' Alix's face lit with excitement she couldn't hide.

But Kathy thought it was just eager interest and said, 'Now you'll be able to see for yourself how gorgeous he is.'

'You think he'll come in here?'

'I should think so; he usually comes to say hello when he gets back.'

'And goodbye when he goes,' chimed in another girl.

It was quite a large office with about a dozen girls and young men, all doing more or less equal jobs, situated on the fifth floor of the building. The directors' offices were on the floor above, so no one saw Rhys as he went up in the lift to see Todd Weston. Alix made for the cloakroom to check her make-up and brush her hair. When she'd last seen Rhys it had still been a mass of short curls, but she wore it longer now, so that it caressed her shoulders in a shining, golden mane. Not having expected to see him, she'd put on normal working clothes: a skirt, and sweater over a shirt, but the skirt was tight enough to outline the slimness of her hips and the sweater a shade of blue that emphasised the sea-blue of her eyes. Anyway, it would have to do.

When Rhys finally came to the office over an hour later, Alix was standing at a filing cabinet over by the wall, and had her back towards him. She heard his voice and began to quiver with excitement so strong she thought her heart would burst, but she didn't turn round. No one had told Rhys that she was working here and she wanted to take him completely by surprise. He worked his way down the room, greeting everyone he knew by name, came to say hello to Kathy. Then he glanced past her at Alix and said, 'You've got a new girl, I see.'

Alix took a deep breath and swung round, her face radiant. 'Hello, Rhys.'

Rhys's eyes widened incredulously. 'Alix?'

With a laugh of pure delight, she ran to him and threw her arms round his neck in spontaneous joy.

He gave a whoop of astonished laughter, and put his hands on her waist to lift her up and swing her round. 'Urchin!' And then he kissed her, right there in front of them all. 'What on earth are you doing here?' he demanded when he straightened up.

'I work here.' She still had her arms round his neck and he his hands on her waist, and to Alix it was the best moment, ever. 'I've been here for months.'

'And no one told me?'

'We wanted it to be a surprise.'

'It was certainly that.' His grey eyes laughed down at her. 'I shall have words to say when I get home.'

'Are you going now?'

'In about half an hour. I've got a car laid on. Want a lift?'

'Of course.'

'OK. Meet me out front.'

He went to let her go but she pulled him closer and stood on tip-toe to murmur in his ear, 'I'm glad you're home, Rhys.'

His eyes met hers for a moment, saw the radiance in their depths. 'Still?' he asked, only half teasingly.

'Still,' she answered with sincerity. 'Always.'

He brushed her lips with his, then said, 'See you later,' and walked out of the office.

'Well!' Kathy exclaimed as soon as he'd gone. 'You're a dark horse. I thought you said you didn't know him.'

Alix came back to earth to find everyone staring at her, which made her blush. 'Oh, no; you never asked me. You just took it that I didn't.'

Some of the others came to cluster round and Kathy gave her a shrewd look. 'You could easily have told us. Why didn't you?'

'I wanted to surprise him.'

'Well, you certainly did that. And you obviously know him *very well*,' one of the men said.

Alix coloured again at the emphasis that had been put on the last two words. 'Oh, yes. I've known him nearly all my life. We live next door to each other, you see.'

Faces cleared and people went back to their desks, a few picked up phones to pass on the tit-bit of gossip. Kathy looked as if she longed to do the same, but instead pulled her chair closer to Alix's and said enviously, 'How fantastic that you know Rhys. God, I'd give anything to live next door to him. But I'd never have been able to keep it secret like that. Do you see much of him when he's home?'

'Oh, yes, lots,' Alix told her, conveniently forgetting the last couple of years. 'We go out together, too.'

'Really? Oh, wow! Just wait till Donna Temple finds out.' And unable to resist any longer, Kathy reached for the phone.

Several curious faces were looking out of windows when Alix was supposed to meet Rhys, but as it happened he was standing in the foyer, talking to another man when she came out of the lift, a man in his forties, not as tall as Rhys but broad and tough-looking. She hesitated but Rhys saw her and beckoned her over. 'This is the surprise I found waiting for me,' he said with a grin. 'Alix, this is Todd Weston. Todd, meet Alix North. I've been pulling her out of scrapes since she was shorter than my knee.'

Alix gave him an indignant look, but smiled as she shook the outstretched hand of the head of the company. 'Hello, Mr Weston.'

'Hello, Alix,' he said with a Canadian accent. 'Isn't that a boy's name?'

'I thought she was a boy the first time I met her,' Rhys said before she could speak.

Todd Weston looked her over and grinned. 'Well, she's certainly changed.'

'So she has,' Rhys agreed, and they both laughed as Alix blushed furiously.

A chauffeur came in to say the car was there so Todd bade them goodbye. 'See you Monday and we'll talk further, Rhys.' And he clapped him on the shoulder before walking away.

Alix glanced up as they waited on the pavement for all Rhys's luggage to be loaded in the car, saw the faces at the windows, and couldn't help hoping, with great satisfaction, that one of them was that of Donna Temple.

They got in the back of the car, the glass screen dividing them from the chauffeur, and Rhys said, 'Well, urchin, how did you get the job?'

'Purely on merit,' she assured him. 'Although your father did find out about the vacancy,' she admitted.

Rhys's eyebrows flickered and he gave her a thoughtful look. 'Did he, now?'

Alix chuckled richly. 'But wasn't it the most perfect surprise?'

'It certainly was; in your letters you just said you'd got a job.'

'Oh, you did read them, then?'

'Of course.'

'But you never bothered to answer any of them,' she pointed out tartly.

'Yes, I did; I sent you postcards from all over the place.'

'Postcards!' Alix exclaimed with such a disgusted expression that he laughed. 'What good are those to a girl?'

'You used to collect them,' Rhys pointed out.

'I didn't *collect* them—I kept yours.'

'What, all of them?'

'Of course.' Alix didn't say that they were among her most treasured possessions, along with the gifts and Christmas and birthday cards that he had given her over the last sixteen years.

Maybe she didn't have to, because Rhys ran a finger along her throat and up to her chin, and said, looking into her eyes, 'You're a funny one, Alix.'

'Why—because I'm so single-minded about you?'

He smiled and gave a small shrug. 'Yes, I suppose so.'

'I don't see why. Some children know what they want to be—a doctor or a dancer or something—from a very early age, and usually everyone thinks that's great and they're given every help and encouragement. Well, it was more or less the same for me. I saw you and I just knew I wanted to be with you,' she said simply. 'I can't help it—that's just the way it is.'

Rhys shook his head at her. 'I was sure you would have grown out of that by now.'

Alix smiled at him, a delightfully mischievous smile that gave her face an elfin quality. 'And I was sure you would have grown *into* it by now.'

That made him give a burst of laughter and there was an arrested expression in his eyes as he looked at her. Her hand was still in his, but now he put his other hand over it. 'Tell me what you've been doing,' he commanded, giving her all his attention.

'I haven't seen you for more than two years; it would take ages to tell you everything.'

'Well, we have plenty of time. Tell me about college.'

So Alix told him, leaning against his arm, her voice and face animated as she recounted experiences and anecdotes, gratified to have his interest, inwardly bursting with pleasure to be near him.

'And did you make lots of friends?' he asked her.

'Oh, yes, loads. Some I see quite often because they work in London, too. And we're all determined to have a big reunion for our whole year in July.'

'Males as well as females?'

'Of course.

'And didn't any of the men at college take your fancy?'

Again she gave him an impish look. 'No, it's OK, Rhys, you don't have to be jealous.'

'There wasn't even *one* man who interested you?'

She shook her head with certainty. 'No, not even one.'

'You're incorrigible,' he grinned.

Alix smiled back at him and moved closer, her eyes drinking him in. After two years he had changed little, although a line at the corner of his mouth seemed to have deepened. She put up a finger to touch it. 'You're starting to get a cynical line here,' she said reprovingly.

'It's old age,' he said flippantly.

'Not experience?'

'Experience?' He raised an eyebrow at the note in her voice.

'Of women.' And she lifted candid blue eyes to meet his.

Rhys's eyes narrowed. 'What's this—office gossip?'

'Yes,' Alix answered, unable to be anything but truthful with him.

She waited for him to deny it, but he merely sat back and said, 'What have you heard?'

'That women fall over you wherever you go.'

'What?' He gave a crack of surprised laughter. 'You surely don't believe that rubbish, do you?'

'Why not? I think you're fantastic so why shouldn't other girls?'

'Well, it isn't true.'

Alix tilted her head to one side to look at him, all wide-eyed innocence. 'You mean you don't go out with other girls when you're away?'

There was a slightly considering look in the grey eyes that met hers, but then Rhys grinned. 'Somehow I don't think you'd believe it if I said I didn't.'

'Of course I wouldn't,' she answered. 'It wasn't only economics I learned at college, you know. I understand that men have to—gain experience of life.'

'Such worldly wisdom in one so young,' Rhys mocked, making her blush and punch his arm.

'You know what I mean,' she scolded.

He smiled down at her, a look of tender affection in his eyes. 'Yes, urchin, I know what you mean. And have you gained some experience of life?'

The colour in her cheeks deepened. 'No. It's different for girls.'

'Not all girls.'

'Perhaps not,' she admitted. 'But it's different for me—because of you.'

Rhys gave a gasping sigh. 'Alix! You shouldn't do this! You're putting too much onus on me.'

She gave him a steady, earnest look. 'Do you want to marry someone else, Rhys?'

'No, but——'

'Not Donna Temple?'

His brows drew into a frown. 'Who told you about her?'

'Everyone knows about you and her. Do you want to marry her, Rhys?'

The frown deepened for a moment, then cleared, and there was a definite note in his voice as he said, 'No, I don't.'

'Or anyone else?'

Amusement was coming back into his eyes. 'Or anyone else,' he agreed.

Alix gave a smile of pure happiness. 'So that's OK.'

'Is it?'

'Of course. You promised to marry me over sixteen years ago, and I'm going to hold you to it. Besides, if you don't want to marry anyone else, then you might as well marry me. Everyone thinks it's about time you settled down.'

'"Everyone" being my parents, I take it?' he guessed shrewdly.

'And me.'

'But what if you meet someone else and fall in love?'

She shook her head in absolute certainty. 'I won't. I'm in love with you.'

That made Rhys frown again. 'And what if I meet someone and fall in love with her?'

Alix gazed at him for a moment, then let a mock-savage look come into her face. Stretching her hands like claws, she said, 'Then I'll tear her eyes out and scratch her to pieces. I'll boil her in oil and grind her bones to dust.'

'Ugh! Nasty.' Rhys shook his head as if in horror, but there was amusement in his face. 'I take it you'd be jealous?'

'Of course I would.' She grew suddenly serious. 'You remember the last time we saw each other, when I was eighteen?' He nodded. 'Do you remember what you said then?'

Rhys gave her a wary look. 'No, but I've a feeling it was probably something as unwise as that incautious answer I gave to a four-year-old imp who pushed her way into my garden—and my life.'

She smiled, liking that, and leaned towards him so that he put his arm round her. 'I wanted you to marry me, then—when I was eighteen, I mean, but you said I'd got to wait until I was no longer a teenager and ask you again. Well, I'm not a teenager any longer, Rhys.'

He pursed his lips, sighed and nodded. 'I was right; it was an unwise thing to say.'

'But you did say it.'

'So I did.'

She looked up at him, her eyes soft and radiant as stars. 'So will you marry me, Rhys?'

For a long moment he didn't speak, then bent to lightly kiss her parted lips. 'You're very special to me, Alix— but when I want to marry a girl, *I'll* do the asking.'

Alix sat back, deep disappointment in her eyes, but then she frowned and said, 'Well, I must say you're taking a hell of a long time about it. A girl could *die* of frustration waiting for you to come home, you know.'

Which unexpected riposte made him give a crack of laughter and completely eased the situation again. His arm was still round her and he gave her a spontaneous hug. 'Urchin, you are something else.'

Which she rightly took as a great compliment. Wisely, then, she changed the subject, asking him about Australia, which lasted until they reached their village.

'Can you drop me off outside your house and I'll walk round to mine?'

'Don't you want to go through the gate?'

Alix shook her head. 'No, your parents will want you to themselves for a couple of hours.'

He raised an eyebrow. 'Only a couple of hours?'

She grinned mischievously. 'We're all having dinner together at my place.'

Rhys gave a mock groan but leaned forward to tell the driver to stop. 'I might have known. What else have they got lined up for me?'

'Well, there's the welcome home party, and your grandparents are coming to visit, and then——'

Rhys raised his hands in protest. 'Enough! Enough! I can't take any more.'

'Well, it's your own fault,' Alix pointed out prosaically. 'You shouldn't be such a lovable hunk.'

'"A lovable hunk"!' Rhys gave her an outraged look. 'I've been called some things in my time, but that... Get out of the car, woman; I'll see you later.'

Alix did so with a chuckle, and walked home whistling; for the first time Rhys had called her woman instead of urchin, which to her mind was a tremendous step in the right direction.

He was home that time for over six weeks, and to Alix it was wonderful because she saw him not only when he came to Kent, but often in London, too. He drove her back to the office on Monday morning, using his own car this time, but she didn't see him for the rest of the day. Her own office seemed to be extra busy all that morning as several members of staff seemed to visit it for little reason. One of them was Donna Temple. She had her dark hair down today, sleekly combed behind her ears and turning up at the ends. And she was wearing a dress that would have cost a whole month of Alix's salary, but which was well worth the money, the way it stressed the length of Donna's legs and curved in to show the narrowness of her waist. Alix was smartly and neatly dressed, but she hadn't yet found her own style, and she knew a moment of envy for the older girl's sophistication.

Donna's eyes swept over Alix when she came into the room, but she talked for several minutes to one of the men about some papers she had with her, and turned to go before apparently noticing Alix and coming over to pause by her desk.

'You must be Alix North, Rhys's little neighbour. Right?'

The other girl's voice was all sweetness but Alix could recognise a put-down when she heard one. 'That's right. And you are...?'

'Donna Temple.'

'Oh, yes, Rhys's little...' She didn't finish the sentence, just let it hang in the air. Behind her Kathy smothered an over-awed giggle, and the smile on Donna's face changed, became fixed.

'Perhaps you were going to say friend,' Donna said curtly, breaking the silence. 'I am a friend of his, yes. I suppose he told you about me?'

Alix shook her head. 'No, *he* didn't mention you.'

'Well, he will. How are you getting on here?' Donna asked, abruptly changing the subject.

'Very well, thank you,' Alix answered warily.

But it seemed that the older girl wanted to be friends because she gave a gracious smile and said, 'Well, if you have any problems, just let me know. Rhys wants you to get on in the firm and I'd be happy to help.'

'Thanks,' Alix answered. 'But I think I can manage on my own. And I don't have any problems.'

The older girl nodded and walked out of the room, all eyes following her.

'Phew!' Kathy exclaimed. 'I rather think our Donna wants you on her side. Probably hopes to get to Rhys's parents through you.'

'If Rhys had wanted her to meet his parents he would have taken her down before now. Anyway, he isn't interested in marrying her,' Alix said with certainty.

'No?' Kathy's eyes grew round. 'How do you know? Did he tell you?'

Belatedly remembering Kathy's love of gossip, Alix thought she'd better be more circumspect, so said, truthfully, 'I was with him most of the weekend and he didn't mention Donna once.'

'Really? How come you were with him?'

'Our parents are the closest friends. We all had dinner together at my house, then his parents gave an open-house party for him on Saturday; one of those whole day things where people come and go the whole time. I was helping with the food and everything.'

'You are *so* lucky, Alix,' Kathy said soulfully. 'How about inviting me down one weekend when Rhys is there?' But then she said, 'Donna must have been really curious about you, just like all the other people who've been wandering in here today.'

For a day or so people continued to be curious about her, but it all died down when Rhys didn't come into the office again. Alix didn't see him for a few days, but then he phoned her at home one evening. 'How about lunch tomorrow?'

'Of course,' Alix agreed immediately, shelving a shopping hour with Kathy without hesitation. 'Where and when?'

'Meet you in the foyer at one. See you, urchin.'

Alix hadn't expected him to meet her in the building, hadn't expected him to take her out in London, if it came to that. Next day she wore a new outfit and was there early, eager to see him as always. But Rhys was a few minutes late, and when he came out of the lift Donna was with him.

The other girl had a possessive hand on his arm and was laughing up at him. Alix felt a harsh rip of jealousy, that was instantly gone as Rhys said, 'Excuse me, Donna. I have a date. 'Bye.' And he smilingly walked over to Alix and kissed her lightly. 'Hello, little one.'

'Hi.' She dropped her voice. 'Am I being used?'

His eyes immediately filled with laughter. 'You could say that.'

'It's going to cost you a really good meal.'

'It will be worth it.'

'She won't let go, huh?' Alix guessed.

'Something like that. But I think she's got the message now.'

'*Good*,' Alix said with feeling, which made Rhys laugh as he tucked her arm in his and took her out to lunch.

The rest of those six weeks were wonderful because Alix knew she had him to herself, socially, that was; he spent a great deal of time in meetings and conferences, and it was eventually announced that he had been made a director in the boardroom game of musical chairs. And he was still only thirty. When he took her out at first Alix thought it was merely to emphasise to Donna that he wasn't interested, but after two weeks the company hummed with the news that Donna had got a new job and was leaving immediately. Whenever Rhys was free he took Alix to the theatre and concerts, to dinner in ethnic restaurants where he laughed at the doubtful face she pulled as she tried food she'd never heard of before, let alone tasted.

Although Alix had known him most of her life there were many things about Rhys that she had yet to discover; he had never treated her as an adult before, so their conversations were different, making her feel closer to him. And he seemed to have changed since she'd seen him last, become a little harder perhaps. For Alix these weeks became a period of learning about Rhys, and her own experience had broadened so that she was able to look at him with more mature eyes. And the same went for him, she supposed, but she had always been completely open and natural with him, so there was less for him to learn.

When he went back to Australia she went to his flat to collect him, so that she could drive him in his car to the airport and then drive it back to Kent, to garage it at his parents' house. His flat was in a modern block with an entry-phone system. Because she was feeling unhappy at his leaving, Alix had bought a lurid witch mask and put it on when she rang the bell.

Rhys's laugh crackled over the intercom. 'A great improvement. Come on up, Alix.'

His bags were all packed and standing ready in the hall.

'How long will you be away this time?' she asked him.

'Not sure. A couple of months, maybe.' His eyes settled on her face. 'Have you ever thought of getting yourself a flat in London instead of commuting every day?'

She thinned her lips expressively. 'Flats in London cost the earth to rent.'

Rhys held up some keys. 'How about using this one, then, while I'm away?'

Alix's eyes widened with pleasure. 'Rhys! Do you mean it? Oh, that would be great, great, great!'

He laughed and tossed her the keys. 'Don't have any rave-ups and don't upset the neighbours. OK?'

'Of course not.'

'Let's go, then.'

They reached the airport and he turned to her. 'Goodbye, urchin.'

Alix swallowed and blinked hard. 'I'm going to miss you, Rhys.'

He put a finger under her chin and tilted her face, looked down at her with strange intentness. 'Then remember this,' he said softly, and bent to kiss her.

At last it was a real kiss, not that of an indulgent friend, but the kiss of a man to a woman. Letting her know masculine curiosity and desire, softly exploring her mouth, drinking in its moist sensuality, deepening to demand a response. At first taken by surprise, Alix was completely still, but then she gave a low moan of wonder and joy, opening her lips to him, finding herself caught in whirling timelessness, clinging to him as she experienced overwhelming sexual need for the first time in her life.

When he lifted his head there were tears of happiness in her eyes.

'Idiot,' he said, and kissed the tears away.

'Wow!' she managed on a choking laugh. 'That was really something!'

He grinned. 'You should get me on a good day.'

'Yes, *please*,' she said fervently.

He laughed and tweaked her hair. 'Goodbye, urchin. Take care of yourself.'

He unloaded his bags, turned to wave to her as he went through the doors. But it was a while before Alix had recovered enough to start the car and drive home.

Alix moved into his flat the next day, enjoying hanging her clothes beside his in the wardrobe, putting her things out as if they were sharing the place. Not that there was much of Rhys's stuff there; he was hardly at the flat long enough to make it look lived in, and he seemed to take most of his clothes with him. She got into bed that night, her thoughts full of him, when the phone rang.

'Hello, Alix.'

'Rhys! How did you know I was thinking about you?'

'Telepathy. You settled in OK?'

'Yes, fine.'

'I forgot to tell you to forward any post.'

'Will do.' A little disappointed, Alix said, 'Is that why you rang?'

'No.' His voice changed a little. 'I called to ask you to marry me.'

CHAPTER TWO

'ALIX? Alix, are you still there?' Rhys demanded when the silence had lengthened and she still hadn't replied.

'Y-yes, I'm here,' she said faintly. Then, on a note of understanding, that was, however, unable to hide the disappointment, 'It was a joke, right?'

'No joke, urchin. I'm asking you to be my wife.' Again there was a long silence. 'Alix, don't do this to me. Is it yes or no?'

From somewhere, out of the overwhelming joy that filled her heart to bursting, out of the dizzying happiness that filled her head, her every sense, Alix was able to say with some dignity, 'I shall have to think about it.'

'You've got two minutes,' Rhys said in amusement.

This time she was silent for only two seconds. 'Yes, of course I'll marry you, you idiot! Oh Rhys, oh Rhys, oh Rhys!' The happiness bubbled in her voice, then changed to awe as the future she'd always dreamed about shone before her. '*Oh, Rhys!*'

'Can't you think of anything else to say?' he complained.

'I'll try.' She gave a watery chuckle.

'And if you start to cry the deal's off,' he warned.

That made her laugh properly. 'I do wish I could see you.' She rolled on to her stomach. 'Tell me where you are,' she commanded. 'I want to picture you there, proposing to me.'

'It's just a hotel room like any other—except that the fridge is bigger to hold all the beer.'

'I'm in your bed,' she told him with satisfaction. 'And I'm wearing the top of a pair of your pyjamas that you left behind. The dark blue silk one.'

'I never wear the tops,' he told her.

'Oh, good. Think how much money we'll save,' Alix said happily.

Rhys chuckled. 'We'll get officially engaged when I get home,' he told her. 'In the meantime keep it under your hat.'

'Can't I even tell the parents?'

'Oh, sure.' His voice changed a little. 'But don't expect them to be surprised.'

'You think they'll have guessed?'

'They knew I didn't stand a chance.'

Alix laughed richly. 'When did you realise?'

'Realise what?'

'That you were in love with me, of course.'

'Oh...' His voice became flippant. 'When you glared up at me and told me you weren't a boy, you were definitely a girl, of course.'

'Really? Was it that long ago for you, too?' Alix's voice was all eagerness.

'No, idiot. I was only kidding. I'll tell you when I get home. OK?'

'OK,' she agreed, a little wistfully. 'Will you write to me—a proper letter?'

'Wouldn't you rather I called?'

'I'd like you to do both. Oh, Rhys. I wish you were home. I wish you were here with me.'

'It won't be long, just a couple of months.' There was a noise in the background. 'Alix, I have to go now. My car's arrived to take me to work.'

'You'll call me tomorrow?'

'As soon as I can. Bye, urchin.'

'Goodnight, Rhys.' Then, experimenting with happiness, 'Goodbye, darling.'

Being an only child, Alix was used to sharing everything with her parents, and it wasn't in her nature not to, so, even though it was almost midnight, she hugged her joy to herself for only a short time before picking up the phone to call them.

'Daddy,' her voice was still breathless with excitement. 'I've got something to tell you. No. No, I haven't been mugged. I'm quite all right. Fine. Yes, I know you told me to be careful.' She raised her voice. 'Daddy, will you please *listen*?' Alix paused till he was quiet. 'I'm going to get married. I'm engaged!' she told him, the thrilled wonder of it still in her voice. But then she frowned. 'No, I am not at a party and I'm not drunk. Of course it's someone you know—it's Rhys.'

She grinned with supreme pleasure as she heard her father excitedly telling her mother. Then of course her mother came on the line, wanting to know every detail. 'Yes, he phoned me from Australia. I know, isn't it wonderful? What do you mean, you're not surprised? I was. But Rhys said you wouldn't be.' She listened, then said, laughing with excitement, 'No, Ma, of course we haven't set a date yet. Rhys didn't even talk about that. We only got engaged half an hour ago, for heaven's sake! Oh, and he said we weren't to tell everyone yet, not till he comes home and makes it official. No, you can't tell Uncle David and Aunt Joanne because I want to tell them myself. No, Rhys had to go to work. OK. Yes. I promise to ring them right this minute. Yes, I am brilliantly, fantastically happy. More happy than it's possible for anyone to be. Yes, tomorrow. Goodnight, Mum. Love to Daddy. Night.'

The next twenty minutes and more were almost exactly identical as Alix told Rhys's parents the news. Next to her own parents, she was closer to them than to anyone, even her own relations, and had always called them aunt and uncle; the knowledge that their relationship was soon to become even closer gave them all the greatest of pleasure. 'We're so pleased, darling,' Aunt Joanne told her. 'We've been looking forward to this day for years.'

Alix accepted their happiness as perfectly natural, quite sure that their pleasure wouldn't have been half so great if Rhys had chosen to marry some other girl. She had been a proxy daughter to them for so long, and now she was to officially become part of their family. Everything was perfect for them all.

It never occurred to Alix that his parents' love for her might have influenced Rhys's decision to propose to her. And it certainly never occurred to her that her own overwhelming love for him wasn't reciprocated a hundredfold. Everything in the world was wonderful—except for the long, long wait for Rhys to come home and claim her as his own.

Keeping her engagement a secret for the next two months was terribly difficult, especially as her happiness shone from her face and was obvious for all to see.

'You're in love,' Kathy accused her when she went into work the next day.

'Yes,' Alix admitted. 'I am.'

'Who with? Who did you meet over the weekend? It must have been love at first sight,' Kathy said enviously.

'Yes, it was. Isn't life wonderful?'

'I thought you were crazy over Rhys,' the other girl said shrewdly.

'Good heavens, what on earth gave you that idea?'

'What's this new man like?'

'Oh, you know—just fantastic.'

More than that she wouldn't say, but her whole outlook changed. Instead of window-shopping outside clothes shops in the lunch hour, Alix now wanted to look at cutlery and linens, at china and saucepans.

'That's boring,' Kathy protested. 'You're too young and attractive to become a *hausfrau*. Anyone would think you were going to live with this guy.'

Alix protested, but was inwardly excited at the idea. Surely that was what Rhys had intended by letting her live in his flat while he was away? When he came back he would just move in with her and they would live together, eventually getting married, eventually having children, and definitely living happily ever after.

The rest of the day went past all too slowly. At the end of it Alix would dearly have loved to have gone home to share her excitement with her parents, but Rhys had said he would phone her again at the flat, so she had to stay in town. Only when he didn't call that evening did Alix remember that he hadn't promised definitely for that night, just said he'd ring as soon as he could. She fell asleep disappointed, and turned down an outing with some of the girls from the office to stay in the next night, but was overwhelmingly glad she had when Rhys rang again, earlier this time, at ten o'clock.

'Hi, urchin. Have you changed your mind?'

'What about?' she asked, deliberately not understanding.

Rhys chuckled. 'Marrying me, of course.'

'Oh, that. No, I guess I'll make do with you.'

'Only two days and the woman's blasé already.'

'Oh, I'll never be that,' Alix assured him, immediately abandoning her mock coolness. 'I told the parents. They were so pleased, Rhys. You wouldn't believe.'

'Oh, yes, I would. They rang me at some Godforsaken hour in the morning yesterday to congratulate me. All four of them. Your father said I should have asked his permission first.'

'He didn't!' Alix exclaimed delightedly. 'What did you say?'

'I told him that if he'd refused to give it you would probably have disowned him.'

She burst into laughter. 'I would, too. Oh, Rhys, I am *so* happy. But I do wish you were here. Do you wish I was there with you?' she asked, expecting a tender reply.

'No, you'd be completely in the way and I'd never get any work done,' he said prosaically.

That made her laugh again. 'When do you think you will be home? I want to know the exact date.'

She could almost hear him shrug. 'Some time at the end of next month; I can't be any more exact than that at the moment, but everything is going well, no hold-ups.'

'Tell me about it.'

'It would take too long, and these calls cost the earth.'

'When will you call again?'

'Some time next week probably.'

'OK. If I'm not here I expect I'll be at home,' she ventured, not wanting him to phone and wonder where she was.

But Rhys merely said, 'Fine. Listen, will you collect a couple of jackets I left at the cleaners? You'll find the ticket in the top drawer of the chest in the bedroom.'

'Do you want me to send them to you?'

'No, just put them in the wardrobe. Thanks. I'll have to go. Take care of yourself, little one.'

'And you, Rhys. I miss you so much. I——'

'And you, urchin. Bye.'

Alix heard the phone go dead and slowly replaced her own in disappointment. She had been about to tell him she loved him but he had been too quick for her. But that was Rhys, brisk and to the point; and anyway there was really no need to tell him because he already knew, there was nothing in the world he could be more sure of.

Rousing herself, she went over to the chest of drawers to look in the top one. Rhys had cleared several of them out for her, but this wasn't one of them. There were a lot of things in it that he hadn't needed to take to Australia: his gold twenty-first birthday watch, several membership cards, a combined address book and diary. Alix fingered the latter, was strongly tempted to look inside but resisted it. Rhys was hers now; she trusted him implicitly and had no wish beyond curiosity to know about his past.

On Friday Alix went home to Kent and had the most marvellous weekend. To be secretly engaged was wildly romantic, but to be able to share the secret, and discuss it with all the parents, was even better. Her mother and Aunt Joanne were already discussing wedding plans, deciding where and when, drawing up lists of guests. Uncle David picked up their combined list and pretended to be terribly shaken. 'Good lord, John!' he said to her father. 'At this rate we're both going to have to work till we're ninety to pay for all this.' But it was said in fun, and they were all as openly delighted as Alix.

The next two months went by agonisingly slowly. Alix didn't go out much in case Rhys rang, which he did a few times, but the calls were, to Alix, frustratingly short. Instead she sat at home and relieved her feelings somewhat by writing very long letters to Rhys, trying to restrict herself to one a week, but often ending up sending two or three. In return, Rhys sent her several postcards, but she didn't receive the letter she had so longed for; a love-letter, her very first from the man she was to marry.

Life became full of excitement again when Rhys at last rang his parents to say he was coming home in just a few days, he wasn't sure exactly when, though. Alix had finally succumbed to Kathy's persuasion and had gone to see a film with her, so missing Rhys's call to the flat, to her bitter disappointment. And when she tried to ring him back someone with a strong Australian accent said he wasn't available. Trying to control her impatience, trying without much success to hide her happiness and excitement, Alix somehow got through the next couple of days, expecting every night to hear from Rhys so that she would know when to collect him from the airport. But on the Thursday afternoon Alix got a call, not from Rhys, but from his mother.

'Rhys is home, dear. He flew into Gatwick this morning, and it was so near home that he just rang and asked me to collect him. He expected to be here last night and surprise us all, but unfortunately his plane was delayed for hours in Singapore.'

'He's home?' Alix didn't know whether to be pleased or disappointed; she'd rehearsed going to meet him so many times in her mind. 'I'll come straight away.'

'There's no point in rushing, Alix dear; he's so jet-lagged that I've made him have a rest. Come at the usual time and we'll all have a celebration dinner together.'

Alix would much rather have had Rhys to herself that evening, that night, here in London, but realised that if he was at home she wouldn't stand a chance. Even though Rhys's mother had told her not to rush back, Alix still wanted time to wash her hair and get ready for tonight, so she decided to ask to leave early anyway. But unfortunately her own boss was away sick that day, so she had to go to the head of the department to ask permission, and also ask to have the following day off.

'I'm owed a day's holiday,' Alix pointed out, but determined to have the day off no matter what.

'That's OK, Alix. Your work is always up to date. Is it——?' He broke off as there was a brief rap on the door and Todd Weston walked in.

'Hi there. Sorry to interrupt.' He glanced towards Alix and smiled in recognition. 'Ah, the girl with a boy's name. Alex, isn't it?'

'You're close. It's Alix,' she corrected him.

'Nice to see you again. How are you?'

'Fine, thank you.'

His eyes settled on her face and he grinned. 'Yes, I can see you are.' He looked towards the head of department. 'Is there some problem?'

'No.' He shook his head. 'Alix just came to ask for tomorrow off. I was just going to ask her if it was something special?'

He was rewarded with the most dazzling smile. 'Oh, yes, it most *certainly* is.'

Both men laughed at her enthusiasm, and Todd said, 'I wonder if I can guess what it is.'

Alix flushed a little but shook her head and wouldn't explain.

The department head said, 'OK, Alix, off you go. See you Monday.'

'Yes. Thank you. Goodbye, Mr Weston.'

'So long, Alix.'

As soon as she was out of the office, Alix rushed to catch the tube and then the train, willing them to go faster and yet faster, her thoughts flying ahead of her.

It was still only half-past four when Alix ran into the house, hugged her mother in excitement, then ran upstairs to spend the next two and a half hours getting ready. Weeks ago she had found the perfect outfit to wear tonight: black silk evening trousers, a beaded black strapless top, and a loose shirt with silver flecks to go over the top. Alix put them on and felt really glamorous. Her hair she wore long and as straight as it would go with so much natural curl in it, and she wore more make-up than she usually did at home. She added some new expensive French perfume, examined herself anxiously in the mirror, then glowed with satisfaction, knowing she looked good.

Both the families had always been so close that it didn't occur to anyone that Alix might feel a little shy at meeting Rhys again in these new circumstances. It didn't even occur to Alix until they were walking along the road to

Rhys's house. But when they had parted they had been merely long-term friends; now they were engaged to be married. She suddenly longed to be alone when she met him, to have time to be at ease with him again. But with parents as close as hers, Alix didn't stand a chance. They were walking along, chatting happily together, wondering how long Rhys would be at home this time, how long in England.

When they reached the door Alix hung back, terribly unsure of herself. Was she supposed to rush into Rhys's arms, to kiss him and call him darling in front of them all? She couldn't do it, not when everything was so new, not when she hadn't yet been alone with him as his fiancée. She didn't know how to act towards him, how she was supposed to behave. Alix wanted to turn and run but Uncle David had opened the door and was ushering them in.

'Rhys is in the sitting-room.'

They all looked at her expectantly, but Alix knew an uncharacteristic moment of panic and couldn't move.

'Alix?' her father said questioningly.

But then suddenly it was all right because Rhys came out into the hall. He glanced at her, but turned first to her mother and father to greet them and receive their congratulations. Then he quite firmly showed the others into the sitting-room and shut the door so that they were alone. The shyness lasted for a moment longer until Rhys raised his eyebrow and said, 'Had second thoughts?'

'Of course not.'

'Then come here, idiot.' And he spread his arms.

She ran into them and he held her close, then looked down at her teasingly. 'Hello, urchin.'

He kissed her, then, a most satisfactory kiss that left her head in a whirl and made her give a long sigh of discovery when he lifted his head. 'I have been waiting for that for *so* long.'

He grinned. 'Well, I'm home now.'

But she hadn't meant that; Alix meant that she had been waiting for her body to feel this aching need when she was close to him, for awakening womanhood. But she put the thought aside for later, and smiled back at him, her eyes alight with happiness.

'Come on, we have to face them some time.'

Taking her hand, Rhys led her into the sitting-room, to be confronted by their parents with raised glasses of champagne. 'To Rhys and Alix! Congratulations, darlings.'

Then there were kisses all around, they were given champagne and Rhys raised his glass in a silent toast to her. Alix knew she was grinning like an idiot but couldn't help it. It was a moment of the most supreme happiness, to be surrounded by those she loved and who loved her, and to know that her dream had come true and she was to spend the rest of her life with the man she had always wanted. Once, during the course of the evening, when they were all seated round the table, laughing and talking, for a strange moment she felt detached from it, as if she was an onlooker, and the silly thought came into her mind that it was all too good to be true. Someone spoke to her, she blinked and shook off the unwelcome thought, promptly forgot it as she leant forward to reply.

A lot of the talk of course was about the wedding and where they would live. 'You must buy a house near here,' both mothers insisted.

'There's plenty of time,' Rhys said in casual protest. 'We're not even officially engaged yet.'

'So when is the announcement to be made?' her father asked.

Rhys looked amused. 'Loading up your shotgun, John?'

He had never called her parents aunt and uncle, he had always seemed too old for that; to him they were John and Valerie, and he spoke to them as equals. Alix thought about calling his parents by their Christian names only but knew that she never would; they were a different generation and that relationship was firmly fixed with the titles she had used for as long as she could remember.

'I'll phone the announcement through to the newspapers tomorrow,' Rhys was saying. 'Have it come out on Monday. Then you'll be able to tell everyone,' he said to the two mothers in amusement.

'My God, just think of the telephone bills,' his father sighed.

It was like that all through dinner and the evening that followed—light, happy. Alix helped to clear the table and when they went back into the sitting-room found that the others had tactfully left her a space beside Rhys on one of the settees. She would probably have sat next to him if their relationship was as it used to be, would probably have frowned mightily if anyone else had taken the place. But, now that she had the right to be beside him, Alix again felt shy and blushed rosily when Rhys put a casual but possessive arm across her shoulders. Tentatively she reached her hand up to hold his, found it held in a strong grip. Alix glanced at her mother and Aunt Jo and found that both women were looking at them with moist, sentimental smiles on their faces, making Alix quickly look away in case she got maudlin, too.

When they left to go home, Rhys again took control, saying as he helped her on with her coat, 'Alix and I are going to take a walk.'

The street was dark and empty. Rhys put his arm round her and walked her down through the village to an open meadow that they had often gone to when they were young: to lie in the long grass and read, to practice tennis shots, for Rhys to teach her about natural history. A place that had long and good memories for them both. He lifted her over the fence, then leaned against it and pulled her to him. This time his kiss wasn't just adult, it was sensuously intimate. He arched her body against his, letting her feel its hardness against her length and his shoulders hunched as his kiss deepened with passion.

Alix returned his kiss ardently, then gave a gasping moan against his mouth as a fierce fire of need grew deep inside her. 'Rhys.' She said his name on a shuddering sigh as he took her mouth by storm, sending her senses whirling. She clung to him, lost, drowning, crying out in delight and yearning as he put a hand low on her hips and held her tight against him. She moved in sensual arousal, her head tilting backwards as he kissed the long length of her throat. She wanted him. Oh, God, she wanted him so much!

But Rhys loosened his hold, raised his head.

Slowly Alix opened her eyes and stared at him. Her breath was panting, unsteady, and her whole body, every nerve, every pore, seemed to be an aching need for love. 'Oh, Rhys, I love you so much,' she said fervently.

He kissed her lightly, then said, 'I have a present for you.'

'A—a present?' she said dazedly.

'Yes. Look.'

He took a small box from his pocket and clicked it open. Inside was a ring. A large stone surrounded by diamonds that seemed to be on fire in the moonlight. A ring of fire, Alix thought fancifully, her mind still stunned and whirling.

'Here let me put it on for you. I hope it fits. I had your mother find out the size.' He took her shaking left hand in his and slipped the ring on to her engagement finger. 'It's an opal,' he told her. 'There was a mine near where I was working and they let me go down and hack this out for you.'

'You found it yourself?' She turned eyes that were as bright as the ring up to him. 'Oh, Rhys!'

'You keep saying that,' he admonished.

She laughed. 'I know. I'm sorry. It's just—just all so overwhelming.'

'I know, kitten.' He gave her a hug. 'So now it's official. You can go ahead and tell your friends. And at work.'

'Oh, wow, I can't wait! Kathy will just die with jealousy. She thinks you're gorgeous, you know.' Rhys laughed but she turned and put her arms round his neck. 'And so do I. Rhys, I'm so happy. Thank you for my lovely ring and for wanting to marry me. Why did you?' she asked in a sudden burst of vulnerability. 'You could have had any girl you wanted.'

'But you're the one I want.' He raised a finger to trace the outline of her lips. 'My sweet, innocent urchin. Always here. So pretty, so untouched.'

She raised a questioning face at that, but he kissed her again and she forgot everything else for several long, wonderful minutes.

When he let her go, Alix gave a shaky laugh. Her hands were gripping the lapels of his jacket to steady herself, although his arm was strong around her.

'What is it?'

She shook her head a little. 'I—I didn't know it would be as—as devastating as this.'

'Good. I'm glad.'

'Glad that it's devastating?'

'Yes, but mostly glad that you didn't know before.'

'There never was and never will be anyone but you,' she said simply.

Putting his hands on her shoulders, Rhys looked deep into her eyes, then said the words her heart had always longed for. 'That's what I love about you, urchin. My sweet little Alix.'

They kissed again, but then it began to rain and they had to turn and hurry back.

'I'll call for you around eleven tomorrow,' Rhys told her. 'We'll go out somewhere, get away from the parents. Goodnight, little one.'

'Goodnight, my love,' she answered, then quickly slipped indoors so that he could go home and not get wet.

Next day they drove down to the coast, found a deserted stretch of beach and walked along at the edge of the sea, both of them with their shoes off and trousers rolled up to their knees.

'I wouldn't mind living by the sea,' Alix remarked as the wind lifted her hair. She laughed. 'My mother keeps on about buying a house in the village.'

'So does mine,' Rhys said with a mock groan.

She put her arm through his. 'Where will we live?'

'Oh, I expect we'll look for a house round here some time. In the meantime you can continue to stay in the flat whenever I'm away and go back to your parents' when I'm in England.'

She lifted a puzzled face to look at him. 'You want me to move out while you're home?' He nodded. 'But——' she flushed a little '—but I thought we could live at the flat together.'

'When we're married we can, sure.'

Alix stood still and put her hands on his arms, looking up at him earnestly but shyly. 'Rhys, I don't mind—that is, I'd like to live with you there *now*. Not—not wait.'

He kissed her lightly, but to her disappointment shook his head. 'The parents would never wear it. And, besides, I want to do it right. Don't you?'

'Yes, I suppose so,' she agreed.

Hearing the reluctance in her voice, Rhys pulled her to him. 'What's the matter?'

'Will we be married soon, then?'

'We have plenty of time, Alix. You're only twenty. We don't necessarily have to rush things because that's what the parents want. Let's enjoy being engaged.' He kissed her lingeringly, and putting his arm round her, walked along at the edge of the sea.

Completely happy again, Alix immediately put all thoughts of living together out of her mind. If Rhys said they were to wait, then that must be the right thing to do. But although her mind accepted it, her body, newly woken to the magic of his caresses, yearned for fulfilment. But not living together didn't necessarily mean that they wouldn't make love. Alix was young and naïve enough to think that because she couldn't wait then Rhys couldn't either.

She would have liked to ask him, but she was still slightly in awe of Rhys, and shy as yet where sex was concerned. The age difference was still there, the ten years that made him a mature man and her an inexperienced girl. It created a barrier of intense inner admiration of him that she had yet to overcome to be completely at ease in their new relationship, to tease and argue with him as she would have done with someone nearer her own age. She was working on it, but at the moment accepted everything he said as right.

They walked for about a mile, until they reached some rocks that barred the way, then returned to the car and sat down on the sand to eat the picnic Rhys's mother had insisted on preparing. Out to sea, the billowing white sails of several yachts appeared, scudding across the waves.

'Do you remember the sailing dinghy I had before I went to college?' Rhys remarked. 'I wouldn't mind getting another boat when I'm finally home long enough to have the time to sail it.'

'When do you think that will be?'

He shrugged. 'Who knows? Todd Weston intends to commute between here and Canada for a couple of years until his father finally retires and he names the person who's going to take over from him in England.' Rhys turned to look at her and said, his voice suddenly intense, 'I want that job, Alix. But at the moment I'm very much the new boy on the board; I've got to work damn hard, concentrate all my time on the company, if I'm to get it.'

'Does that mean going away a lot?' Alix asked, trying not to let her deep disappointment show.

'Probably.'

'But when we're married—won't they let you stay at home more?'

'If I get the job I'll be able to stay in England most of the time; send other people abroad.'

'Then you *must* get it,' she said fervently. 'What can I do to help?'

Rhys gave a crack of laughter. 'That's my girl!' He lay back against a sand dune and pulled her down beside him. 'Having you working for the company is already a great help. You're bright and intelligent, Alix, you should do well there. And now that we're engaged you'll be invited to a lot of company functions; it will be useful that you already know all the staff.'

'Really? That will be great. I'll get to know every single person there,' she promised expansively.

Rhys smiled at her, but then his eyes darkened and he sought her lips. His tasted cool from the breeze and salt from the sea, but lit an immediate flame deep within her. Alix returned his kiss hungrily, opening her mouth for him, putting her arms round his neck, her fingers running through his hair. Rhys made a growling sound in his throat and pulled her down on top of him. She could feel the hardness of his body and it excited her unbearably. Alix groaned and kissed him fiercely, so fiercely that Rhys gasped and half turned so that she was beside him again.

Alix had on a denim shirt, knotted loosely at her waist. Rhys pulled the knot undone and with expert fingers unbuttoned the shirt. His hand felt hot on her skin, setting it on fire, burning its way up to the straps of her bra, pulling them down. He kissed her shoulders, the hollows below her throat, let his lips trail across her skin. His hand was still on her waist, but she didn't want it there, her body *ached* to be touched, caressed. She had never known such longing, such desperate need. '*Rhys*.' She said his name on a note of entreaty.

Raising his head he looked down at her flushed face, saw the hunger in her eyes and parted lips, and understood. His hand went round her back, unclipped her bra and took it off. His eyes went over her, taking in the beauty of her softly rounded breasts, firm with the elasticity of youth, the small nipples already aroused.

'You're beautiful, Alix,' he told her, his voice thickening. 'Exquisite.'

'Touch me,' she said urgently. 'I want you to touch me.'

He smiled a little and sat up so that he was leaning over her. Stretching out his hands, Rhys gently cupped her breasts and began to caress them. Alix shuddered and closed her eyes, unable to bear the exquisite agony of it. She thought that she would never know such ecstasy as when he toyed with her nipples, hard and thrusting under his fingertips, but then he bent his head to kiss them and she knew that she had been wrong. Her cry of pleasure rose across the beach and echoed across the sea. She put her hands on his head, holding him there, never wanting this consuming joy to stop. Rhys's breathing grew harsh, uneven, and he held her so tightly that he left marks on her skin. Raising his head he stared at her, panting, the deep darkness of desire in his eyes.

He began to push himself off her but she caught hold of him, the basic craving for fulfilment drowning out every other thought. 'Rhys! *Please*.'

His eyes were on her face as he took several deep, ragged breaths, but then he shook his head. 'Not now. We have plenty of time.' Sitting up, he pushed back his hair, then leant back against the sand dune.

Alix sat up uncertainly, her body trembling, unable to recover so easily.

'Come here.' Rhys held her shirt for her to put on but left it open, then leaned her back against him. Putting his arms round her, he again cupped her breasts, but his hands were gentle and undemanding now. Kissing her neck, he said, 'Has anyone ever touched you there before?'

'Once,' she admitted. 'A boy at college took me to a party and groped me on the way home.'

'Is that all he did?' Rhys's voice sharpened.

'Oh, yes. I ditched him and walked the rest of the way alone.'

'Good for you. Tell me his name. I'll kill him.'

She laughed, liking that, liking the way he was holding her. It was so *intimate*, as exciting, but in a different way, as when he had kissed her before. It was such a loving thing to do, and so possessive. In that moment Alix felt truly engaged, realised that she had promised herself, her body, to this man to do with as he liked, to handle as and when he wanted. And it was for her to respond, to give willingly and ardently, or just to lie back and let him toy with her as he was doing now.

Glancing down, seeing his hands on her, made her flush, but it excited her, too. But his earlier question made her wonder how many women he had held like this. Suddenly turning, she kneeled up in front of him, her breasts tip-tilted, still hard. Rhys looked at her, his mouth curving, eyebrows raised.

'Do you like my—me?' she demanded.

'Your breasts are beautiful, Alix; I've already told you,' Rhys assured her.

'Better than Donna Temple's?'

He burst out laughing, the rich masculine sound of it drowning the noise of the sea. Alix's face immediately flamed bright red with embarrassment and she hit out at him. 'Don't you *dare* laugh at me!'

Still laughing, he grabbed her wrists, and jerked her forward so that he could put his arms round her. 'Alix! What a question! Only you could ask it.'

'Well?' she demanded angrily.

'You are beautiful and gorgeous and exquisite and lovely. More beautiful than any girl I've ever known. There! Happy now?'

Mollified, she looked into his face and suddenly laughed with him. 'For a minute I was jealous.'

'You have no reason to be. You're the girl I want, urchin. The only one I've ever asked to be my wife.'

She sighed, content and happy again. Bending forward, Rhys very deliberately kissed each of her breasts, then tossed the wispy laciness of her bra over to her. 'Better get dressed, Alix; I can see some people coming.'

She did so, then packed up the picnic. A glass had rolled into the sand. Unthinkingly, Alix picked it up with her left hand, too late realising that she had her ring on. Some sand had gone on to it and she blew it off, then wiped it carefully with her handkerchief. Lifting her hand she let the sun shine on the diamonds, moved it so that the opal caught the light. 'Mummy loved the ring,' she told Rhys. 'But it was so strange; when I showed it to

Daddy this morning he said he'd heard that opals were unlucky.'

'An old wives' tale,' Rhys assured her.

She laughed happily. 'Or in this case, an old husband's tale.'

They cleaned the sand off their feet, the way they had a hundred times before when visiting the beach, and got in the car to drive home. Alix's nerves still tingled, her mind was full of the wonder of his caresses, and although she had wanted to go on so much, she knew now that he had been right to stop. It hadn't been the right time or place. But what they had done had been wonderful, a deeply exciting foretaste of the wonder that was to come. Soon, she felt confident, Rhys would arrange for the time and place to be right; perhaps they would go away for the weekend somewhere, and then they would become lovers at last.

Alix was so happy that day; there was no cloud in the sky or in her heart, nothing to warn her what the future would hold.

CHAPTER THREE

THE next few days were busy, but especially happy ones. On Saturday there was a family party at Alix's house to celebrate the engagement, and on Sunday they all went over to Rhys's grandparents' place to a buffet lunch for all his family. Not that there was much difference between the two sets of relations really; they had all known each other for so long that it all seemed like one big family, and now, to Alix, would be. The only drawback during those two days was the number of times Alix was asked when the wedding was going to be, but by the end of them she had her answer off pat: 'We're going to enjoy just being engaged for a few months first.'

The weekend had been good, but going to work the next day was sublime. Rhys drove her up and parked in his reserved space in the company's underground car park. 'If you use the car while I'm away you might as well use this space,' he told her.

Alix laughed. 'That will make all the junior execs green with envy.' She had dressed with extra care today, putting on a navy and white full skirt with a navy top and short-sleeved jacket, both summery and businesslike. Kathy was already in the office when she walked in. Going up to her desk, Alix leaned her left elbow on it and rested her chin on her hand. 'Good morning, Kathy,' she said pointedly.

Kathy looked up from the newspaper she was reading. 'Hello, Alix. Did you have a good wee——?' She broke off to give a shriek. 'What a fantastic ring! Who gave—Alix! Is it an engagement ring?'

'It certainly is,' Alix answered gleefully, standing up and extending her hand so Kathy could have a closer look.

'It's gorgeous. Are you really engaged? When did this happen? Is it that new man you've been going out with and won't talk about? But you've only known him a couple of months.'

'So many questions,' Alix laughed. Then she blushed a little and said, 'Actually, I've a confession to make. There isn't anyone new. I've been engaged for the last couple of months, but we only made it official this weekend.'

Kathy frowned. 'Not someone new? Then who?' Her mouth slowly fell open. 'Alix! You're not—no, you couldn't be. It's not—it's not Rhys?'

Alix gave a huge grin and nodded excitedly.

'*You're going to marry Rhys Stirling*?' Kathy's voice rose in excited amazement, and everyone else in the office turned to stare. 'Oh, wow! I can't believe it. How fantastic! Oh, Alix, you are so lucky!' She came round the desk and gave Alix an impulsive hug. 'But how did you keep it so quiet? Tell me *everything*.'

But the other girls were crowding round, eager to know, wanting to see her ring. It was one of the greatest moments of Alix's life. She stood among them, laughing, explaining, receiving their congratulations, aware of the envy of many of them, inevitably saying that she and Rhys hadn't set a date yet. People came into the office all morning to wish her happiness, and at lunchtime, when she went down to the foyer to meet Rhys, the day was crowned when Todd Weston came with him and gave

Alix a kiss of congratulation and insisted on taking them both out to lunch.

Alix was a little overwhelmed by Todd Weston at first, but he was such a larger-than-life character, very expansive and friendly, and full of anecdotes, that he soon had Alix at ease and laughing, and insisted on her calling him Todd. He was in his mid forties, she guessed, pleasant-looking, with a wide grin, and reddish hair that was starting to recede. He told her about his home town in Canada where he still had a house, said that Rhys must bring her out for a visit, and treated her, as he treated Rhys, as an equal. As an only child, Alix was used to being in adult company, and Todd's ease of manner soon had her talking to him as she would to her parents' many friends. She told him about some of the funny things that had happened in college, making them both laugh.

'Hey, you know something,' Todd said as they were having coffee. 'I'm looking for a junior PA, someone who can take over from my present personal assistant when she's ill or on holiday. Someone who doesn't mind travelling when necessary and can act as hostess when I entertain, look after prospective clients, that kind of thing. You think you could do that, Alix?'

Her eyes opening wide in surprise, Alix said, 'Why, yes, of course, but...' She looked at Rhys in some consternation. 'Did you know about this?'

'Not a word.' He looked at Todd. 'I've an idea you've only just this minute thought of it.'

Todd laughed. 'More or less. But Brenda, my London-based PA, doesn't like flying since she had a bad scare a year or so ago. And there's no way I can get her into a helicopter to reach some of the more remote places where the company's working. And the PA in Canada is almost as old as my father and won't move out of the office. So what I need is a travelling assistant and secretary. So how about it, Alix? Fancy the job?'

'It sounds fantastic, but at the moment I'm only a lowly assistant in the estimating department,' she pointed out. 'It would be a big advancement.'

'But your work is good; I've checked on that. In your quarterly report your boss said that you know your way round a computer better than some of the senior secretaries. And that you're practical and intelligent. That's the kind of person I want. And someone who doesn't mind flying, of course,' Todd added with a grin.

Alix smiled back, but said, 'It's really very kind of you. I'm very flattered. But I really don't know.' Again she glanced at Rhys for guidance.

He looked at Todd, a small smile on his lips. 'I take it you would be flying to some of the places where I'll be working?'

'Could well be,' Todd agreed.

'In that case, I think it will be a very good idea.' Reaching out, he put his hand over Alix's. 'It will give us more opportunities to see each other.'

'But when we get married?' she reminded him, wishing that they were alone to discuss this.

'That won't be for some while yet, and this will be a very good way for you to travel and see something of the world first. That aspect has been worrying me,' Rhys admitted.

It hadn't worried Alix; if she was going to travel then she would much rather have done it in his company. But as he'd said; this way she would perhaps be able to see him sometimes when he was away during their engagement, and possibly even the first year or so of their marriage. Then, hopefully, he would take over Todd's job in England and they would be able to settle down, buy a house, and have children. Alix remembered that she'd offered to help him get that job; maybe this was a way that she could do it. So she gave Todd a brilliant smile and said, 'In that case, I'd love to do it.' Her conscience smote her. 'But won't everyone think that you've only offered it to me because of Rhys?'

'Don't worry; it will be advertised within the company and you'll have to apply for it, the same as everyone else.' Todd winked at her. 'But I think you stand a pretty good chance—I need someone without ties, that I can trust. And your being engaged to Rhys is a definite plus because he understands the amount of travel the work involves.'

The position was duly advertised by the personnel department, Alix applied, and within six weeks was moving into a small office on Todd's floor. Rhys had gone away again by then, to Saudi Arabia this time, to try to get an order to build a new oil refinery. Alix had been desperately sad to see him go. The three weeks he had been home, on holiday, had been wonderful. The only drawback had been that Alix had to work because she hadn't been at the company long enough to accrue more than a few days' leave. These she had spent with Rhys, sailing mostly, and she had seen him after work, too. But he had always either put her on a train or else driven her back to Kent, then left her at her door after kissing her goodbye.

But every time he kissed her the need for him grew, consuming her body like a forest fire.

When they went out together in London, Alix always expected Rhys to take her back to his flat to make love to her. But they never went there. Sometimes when he kissed her goodnight in the car his breathing would quicken and he would caress her breasts, driving her crazy, but then he would draw back, and the frustration would deepen.

It drove her mad, too, wondering why he didn't take the love she was so eager to give him. But when he went away and she lay alone in his bed in the flat, she had plenty of time to think, and it gradually dawned on her that Rhys was holding back for her sake. And maybe holding back from getting married for the same reason. She had told him that she had always loved him and always would, but working in London had shown her that she had led a pretty sheltered life. Because she'd mixed always with adults, she was old for her age in some ways, especially socially, while in others, because she'd had eyes for no one but Rhys, she was very immature and inexperienced. To Rhys that must be very evident. She'd told him that her feelings for him would never change, but maybe he wanted to give her the time to be absolutely sure of that.

Once, when they were out together, Alix remarked that a couple they knew were splitting up. 'It's such a shame, because they were childhood sweethearts.'

His eyes settled on her face. 'People grow up, change, want more out of life. They find that just being married isn't such a happy ending after all.'

Glancing up, she saw the seriousness in his eyes. 'You mean,' she said slowly, 'that people should look beyond marriage before they make up their minds?'

'Marriage should be a beginning, not an end.'

She nodded. 'Yes, I see that. But they couldn't have loved one another enough.' Smiling at him, Alix leaned her head on his shoulder. 'Not like us,' she said with absolute certainty.

But now, alone, she remembered that conversation, and became positive it was to give her time to see more of life that Rhys was holding back. But if so, why had he wanted to get engaged at all, then? The answer to that one came easily enough: because he was old enough to know his own mind and was quite sure that he loved her. So he had asked her to marry him to make sure that he didn't lose her. But, having done so, he didn't want to deprive her of the opportunity to see some life for herself before she settled down to marriage. So he was being truly unselfish, controlling his own needs, so that she wouldn't feel coerced in any way.

Having reasoned that out to her satisfaction, Alix felt far better. She was still achingly frustrated, but could exert enough mind over matter to control it—except when Rhys rang and she poured out her longing for him. 'I miss you so much,' she would sigh into the phone. 'So much. If only you were here, beside me.'

When she began to work for Todd, though, she had to work far longer hours, and concentrate so hard, that she was glad there was nothing else to think about. There was so much to learn; the job was certainly no sinecure. Todd kept a tight hold on the company, knew everything that was going on, and often worked far into the evening. Brenda, his PA, who had taken over when Donna Temple had left, accepted Alix with pleasure, glad to be released from the terrors of flying, and helped her as much as she needed. There were a few remarks about nepotism and favouritism from failed candidates when it was announced that Alix had got the job, but her boss had given her a glowing report and told everyone so, and her own innate charm and friendliness soon dispelled any ill-feeling.

She was amply rewarded for the hard work when, about three weeks later, Todd took her with him to Saudi, to find out the latest on the project Rhys was working on. Todd used the company jet, a smallish plane that carried only about a dozen passengers, and which he piloted himself, the official pilot sitting beside him and acting as navigator. But when the latter came back into the cabin for a while Todd called Alix forward and let her sit in the co-pilot's seat.

'Ever flown in a small plane before?' he asked her.

She nodded eagerly. 'There's a flying club near where we live. A friend of Daddy's learnt and took us up a couple of times. We didn't go anywhere though, because he hadn't taken his navigation tests, so we just went round and round the field.'

Todd laughed. 'Think you'd like to fly this one?'

Her face grew wistful. 'Oh, would I! It's beautiful.'

'Take hold of the controls; feel what it's like.'

Alix did so, holding the yoke gingerly at first, nervously aware of the power under her hands. But Todd was still holding his control yoke so there was no danger. He tilted the plane a little, first to one side then the other, so that she could feel what it was like. Alix asked him questions about the controls, enjoying every minute. 'You're a natural. Maybe I'll arrange for you to have flying lessons,' Todd told her when the pilot came back.

She laughed happily, wound up with excitement at the thought of seeing Rhys again. He was waiting for them at the airport in Riyadh, looking tall and tanned, and, to Alix's eyes, utterly fantastic. She ran into his arms and he gave her a hug but didn't kiss her, even drew back when she went to kiss him. Alix gave him a startled, reproachful look, but he bent to whisper, 'They don't do that kind of thing in public here. We'd be arrested on the spot if I kissed you the way I want to.'

That made her laugh, and Rhys grinned back at her before turning to greet Todd. Rhys had a car waiting and took them to a hotel to check in and change before driving them out to the site of the new oil refinery.

'We have some foreign competition for the job,' Rhys told Todd. 'We've submitted our plans and estimates, but things take time here, and it's a matter of protocol, as much as anything. Usually you have to wait a couple of days just to see the minister in charge to find out how things are going. Your coming should be a help. There's a reception at the British Embassy in a couple of days and the minister will be there. I've arranged for the three of us to go. Once you've met the minister officially he'll have to see you. Then you can do some pushing for an answer.'

They talked some more, Alix sitting in the back seat, listening, and taking notes whenever Todd threw a sentence at her over his shoulder. She was getting used to him now, knew when something was an instruction for her or a reminder for him.

'How's she shaping up?' Rhys asked Todd, but his eyes on Alix in the driving mirror.

'Just great. And she loves flying; I'm gonna have her take flying lessons.'

Rhys laughed. 'To hell with the typing, if she's as nuts as you over flying, is that it?' He glanced back at Alix. 'Todd only comes out to the sites so he can fly the plane.'

She leant forward and put her arms on the back of the seats. 'You're a flying freak, huh?'

'Aw, he's given my secret away,' Todd grinned.

Alix chuckled, liking the way they joked with one another, thinking that if the two men were on such good terms, then Rhys stood a really good chance of taking over from Todd. Being Todd's assistant meant that she had obviously learnt quite a lot about the company hierarchy. His father, old Mr Weston, was now in his seventies, but was only reluctantly and slowly handing over to Todd. To his credit, Todd was being very patient about this, gradually taking on more on the Canadian side, but unable yet to be there permanently. Which meant a great deal of commuting and astronomical fax and phone bills.

Todd didn't seem to mind the travelling, but Alix had learnt from Brenda that it was playing hell with his personal life. His wife and two children were at present based in England and his wife wanted to stay there at least until the children had finished primary school. Todd, though, wanted them to move back to Canada, which would help persuade his father to retire completely. The old man seemed to think he ought to keep going so that Todd could be with them in England.

'No one knows for sure,' Brenda confided, 'but I wouldn't be at all surprised if Todd's wife hasn't said something to old Mr Weston; he seemed quite willing to retire not that long ago, then changed his mind.'

'Would she do that?' Alix had asked, surprised.

'I wouldn't put it past her,' Brenda answered with a sniff.

Alix had met Todd's wife. She came to the office one day, shortly after Alix had got the job, and Todd had introduced them. Her name was Lynette and she was English. She was a rather short woman but with a good figure, and wore the most elegant clothes.

'So you're the girl that Rhys has been keeping so secret all this time,' Mrs Weston remarked, looking her over. She smiled at Alix, but the smile didn't quite reach her eyes. 'Well, I hope you'll both be very happy. You must come to the house soon and have dinner.'

'Thank you, we'd love to. But I'm afraid Rhys is away at the moment,' Alix answered, rightly guessing that the invite wasn't for her alone.

Mrs Weston nodded. 'As soon as he comes back, then. He's always such an asset at a party. Well, good luck in the new job. Oh, and try, if you can, to stop this husband of mine overworking.' And she put a possessive hand on Todd's shoulder.

Mrs Weston left soon afterwards, and Alix had the distinct impression that she had only come to look her over. Out of curiosity, Alix supposed. There could certainly be no cause for jealousy when she was engaged to Rhys. Only then did it occur to her that that was probably the reason Todd had picked her for the job in the first place.

Back in Riyadh, the capital of Saudi Arabia, the three of them had dinner together, but then Todd tactfully left Rhys and Alix alone, if you could call sitting in a hotel lounge full of other people being alone. Rhys obviously didn't because he took her hand to help her to her feet from the low couch, and said, 'Let's go for a drive.'

It was very hot outside after the air-conditioned coolness of the hotel. Rhys had an American convertible car and the breeze was gorgeous as they drove around the town. The city was built in a huge oasis so there were lots of palm trees sheltering the beautiful white buildings of the palace and university. Alix admired them all, but was impatient to be in Rhys's arms. He drove through an ornate gateway in the walls of the city and then through the acres of date gardens which surrounded it until they came to the open desert. Only then, where there was no one to see, did he pull off the road and park. But even then he put the top up before he turned to kiss her.

His lips were hard, urgent, and for several long, intoxicating minutes Alix knew that he'd missed her, that there was desire in the hands that fondled her, in the mouth that crushed hers with passion. 'Sweetheart,' Rhys murmured against her mouth. 'My sweet little urchin.'

'I'm too old for you to call me that any more,' Alix told him, her fingers in his hair. 'I'll soon be twenty-one.' She drew back a little to look at the lean lines of his face in the clear moonlight. 'Will you be able to get back for my birthday? My mother wants to have a party for me.'

'Your mother is always having parties.'

'I know,' Alix laughed. 'But so is yours. Any old excuse will do. But it would be nice; I could show you off to all my college friends who haven't met you yet.'

'So that's the only reason you want me there, is it?'

'You know it's not,' Alix said earnestly. Putting her hands on either side of his face, she looked deep into his eyes, then bent to kiss him lingeringly. 'I adore you,' she whispered, her lips gently brushing his. 'I long to be with you, to be a part of you.'

His arms tightened around her, crushed her against him, and Rhys would have kissed her again but a truck came along the road, its headlights lighting the car.

Immediately Rhys drew back, sitting sideways in his seat, screening her, but even so the truck driver sounded his horn mockingly, as if he knew.

'Damn him,' Rhys said feelingly.

'Couldn't we go back to the hotel?'

'It might be an idea; this is hardly the country for showing you how much I've missed you.'

'No, I mean... Couldn't you show me, back in my room?' Alix suggested tremulously.

Rhys sighed and leaned forward to kiss her. 'Temptress! I wish we could, urchin, but I've got to be careful. Getting the contract for the oil refinery is too important to risk a diplomatic incident.'

Alix was disappointed but had expected as much, so she said teasingly, 'You don't think making love to me would be worth it?' And she slipped her hand inside his shirt to caress his chest, twirling her fingers in his hairs, making his nipples stand on end.

He groaned against her neck, caught her hand to stop her. 'It might at that,' he said thickly. 'Who taught you to do that?'

'Wouldn't you like to know,' she taunted, but was immediately taken aback when his hand tightened sharply on her wrist.

'Who?' Rhys demanded in a tone that couldn't be denied.

Alix drew back a little, not at all frightened and rather elated. She hadn't known before that she had the power to make him jealous. But she didn't use it, instead saying, 'No one taught me; I saw it in a film. Do you like it?'

'Of course I do, idiot. But now isn't the time or the place. Now I'm really going to have to get back to the hotel so I can have a cold shower.'

She laughed, pleased with these new powers: to turn him on until he groaned, to make him jealous. OK, so they couldn't make love, but finding out these things went a long way to compensate for it.

The next day she was left to sunbathe in the privacy of the hotel pool while Todd and Rhys tried to set up a meeting with the minister, but on the following day Alix found out yet a third thing about herself. They all went to the reception at the British Embassy and Alix, forewarned by Brenda, wore a long, straight skirt and a lacy top with long sleeves and a high neck in a pale peach colour that matched the tones in her engagement ring. It was a far more sophisticated outfit than Alix was used to wearing, so she got the hairdresser at the hotel to put her hair up into a pleat with a few little tendrils of hair loose around her ears and neck.

She liked the effect and so did Rhys when she joined him and Todd in the foyer. Rhys's eyes widened and an arrested look came into them. He took her hand and leaned forward to say in her ear, 'You're becoming quite beautiful, urchin.'

Todd complimented her, too, and Alix glowed with happiness. She felt great being with Rhys when he wore his white dinner jacket, he looked so good, and Todd, too, was smart in his. Each of them smilingly offered her an arm and they all three walked out to the waiting car.

They drove to the embassy, where she expected to just blend in the background, but Todd introduced her to several of the Arab guests, who seemed charmed by her, and she found instead that she became quite a centre of attention. At first she thought it was because she was introduced as Rhys's fiancée, but several lonely young

men, expatriates working in Saudi, wanted to meet her
for her own sake. In fact, Rhys had to elbow his way
through them to reach her, and determinedly walked her
away to the other side of the room. 'If you get any
lovelier,' he said lightly, 'I shall have to issue you with
a chastity belt.'

That made her laugh, but she slipped her arm in his
and said, 'I've a better idea.'

'What's that?'

'Marry me straight away and take me with you
wherever you go.'

Rhys gave her one of his lazy, intimate smiles, that
always turned her heart over, he looked so devastating.
'Looking at you tonight, that idea seems more attractive
by the minute.'

But though he'd said it, when Rhys came home from
Saudi Arabia, the contract in the bag, he made no move
to set a date for their marriage. And he'd missed her
twenty-first birthday, to Alix's deep disappointment. The
negotiations had reached a crucial stage and he just
couldn't leave. A great bouquet of flowers arrived from
him on the day, and he phoned and sent her the most
beautiful bracelet, but his absence spoiled her birthday.
How could she celebrate when Rhys wasn't there to share
it with her? Or to show off to her friends; Alix had very
much been looking forward to that, too.

It was a disappointment, but working for Todd had
taught her how delicate negotiations to get a contract
could be, so she tried to understand. And she tried to
understand when Rhys was almost immediately sent off
to Australia again to deal with some problem that had
arisen with the project there.

Learning to understand became almost a way of life. Whenever Rhys came home she would confidently expect him to tell her to name the day for their wedding, but there always seemed to be some contract he had to try and get or problem he had to deal with, which meant him jetting off to some new country. Or else she was away somewhere with Todd, who was having problems of his own. His father had put more work in his hands, enough to warrant going to live in Canada again, but his wife had refused point-blank to leave England. While he tried to persuade her to change her mind, he commuted endlessly across the Atlantic, often taking Alix with him. They usually went by scheduled flights, and Alix began to feel that she lived either in London or Toronto airports; she certainly seemed to see more of them than anywhere else.

She wasn't the only one that was flying; time flew by, too. All too quickly. Alix filled some of her spare hours with cookery lessons, because Rhys had suggested it. She was able to afford decent clothes now, and developed a chic, elegantly casual style of her own, filling Saturdays when she was alone by wandering round the stores in whatever country she happened to be in. She had stopped buying household stuff; the spare room at home was full of it and her mother had told her to stop or there would be nothing that anyone could buy her for wedding presents. Which they both knew was a tactful way for her to call a halt.

Christmas came and went, with Rhys managing to get home for only a few days. Days in which she had to share him with his parents and relations and had little time alone with him. When they were alone he was as devastating as ever, setting alive all the aching yearning and frustration all over again. She wanted him so much. She told him so, but he refused to be rushed into a hurried wedding and brief honeymoon.

'We're going to do this properly,' he told her again. 'You know that's what the parents want. You don't want to disappoint them, do you? We'll be married as soon as I take over from Todd.'

But things didn't work out for Todd. He had to give in to his wife, and promised her one more year in England. But it meant he had to put someone else temporarily in charge in Canada while he based himself in England again. For Alix it was a bitter disappointment, for both sets of parents, too. But Rhys, when she told him over the phone, seemed strangely philosophical about it.

'It's only for another year, urchin. Todd will keep his word, you'll see. If he's given his wife a time limit, then he'll keep to it.'

'But what about us? I don't want to have to wait another whole year,' Alix protested, almost in tears.

'It isn't all bad news, Alix. Todd has promised me that I'll take over for him.'

'He has? Oh, that—that's good.' She tried to be pleased, but a thought occurred to her and she said, 'Did you already know about this, Rhys?'

'That he was going to stay on for another year? Yes. But don't get angry that I didn't tell you; Todd didn't want anyone else to know at the time.'

'You're very loyal to Todd,' Alix remarked, unable to hide the bitterness in her tone.

'It's part of the job. You know that. You're as much involved with the company as I am now.'

'Yes,' Alix agreed. But though she loved the job she loved Rhys a whole lot more, and she felt that he ought to feel the same. 'But can't we get married anyway? I don't see any point in waiting.'

But she couldn't persuade him; the most she could get out of him was a promise to discuss it when he got home, probably at Christmas again.

It seemed that she wasn't the only one bringing pressure to bear on Rhys; his parents, too, had been urging him to settle down, with the result that when he came home there was an obstinate line to his mouth. Alix recognised it and immediately gave up any idea of urging him to set a date. She realised she would have to change tactics and her first thought, remembering how he had reacted before, was to make him jealous. But when she reviewed all the men she knew and might use in her mind, she at once saw that there wasn't one of them that Rhys wouldn't look at and immediately know what game she was playing. There just wasn't one who came even close to having his magnetism, his masculine appeal. So, driven to desperation, she got him alone and tried to seduce him.

They were in London. Rhys was staying in his flat and had arranged for them to go out to dinner with Todd and his wife and another couple, all meeting up at the restaurant at seven-thirty. Alix was supposed to meet Rhys at his flat at seven, but instead, at six-fifteen, she took a taxi round to the flat and let herself in with her key. Rhys was in the shower, whistling. Nothing could be better. Summoning up all her courage, Alix swiftly took off all her clothes, crept into the bathroom, and got into the shower behind him while he was washing his hair, his eyes blinded by soap.

His body was beautiful, so lean and powerful, his shoulders wide and his arms muscled. He was still tanned, except for the one white patch that his swimming trunks had covered. Soap ran down him in white rivulets. Her body tense, shaking with nerves, Alix put her arms round him, lifted her hands and began to massage the soap over his chest.

Rhys froze in stupefied surprise, then threw the soap aside as he whirled round to face her. 'Alix!' He said her name in thunderstruck amazement.

'Hello, Rhys.' She gave him a vivid smile, her eyes eager, but a little afraid of his reaction. Stepping forward under the cascading water, she put her hands on his shoulders and reached up to kiss him.

His hands covered hers, and for a terrible moment Alix thought that he was going to push her away. He did in fact make a movement to do so, but then Rhys's eyes travelled down from her face and his hands tightened convulsively as his gaze went on down her body.

Taking full advantage, Alix found his lips and kissed him hungrily, the water on her hair, streaming down her back. Rhys returned the kiss avidly, putting his hands on her shoulders and holding her against him. His body hardened, so quickly, so much, that it startled her. She stepped back a little, wanting to look at him but embarrassed to do so. Instead she looked into Rhys's eyes, a flush of colour creeping into her cheeks. His face was tense with need, dark hunger in his eyes. Stooping, he picked up the soap and began to rub it over her, his lips finding hers again as he did so, bending her back against his left arm so that he had the freedom of her body. Soon he dropped the soap again and used his hand to massage the lather over her, from her neck to her knees, but concentrating on all the curves in between.

Alix began to writhe and moan with desire, not knowing that her body could be so roused, that it was possible to feel such excitement, such hunger.

Suddenly Rhys pulled her to him again, kissed her lips, her breasts, on down her body. Alix cried out, her head thrown back, fingers digging his shoulders, unable to bear it. 'Rhys! Rhys!' She cried out his name in an agony of frustrated hunger.

He straightened, looked down at her for a moment as she lay back in his arms, eyes wild, her nipples hard and thrusting. Reaching out, he turned off the shower, then deliberately began to explore her, finding the sensitive areas that Alix had read about but never before known she had. Her breath came in small, gasping pants, and she moaned under his hand. Then could stand it no longer and broke free, only to throw herself against him, moving her hips against his, wanting, wanting, wanting. A shudder ran through him and Rhys gave a gasping groan. Picking her up in his arms, he carried her through into the bedroom, dropped her as she was, soaking wet, on to the bed, stood over her for a moment.

Alix looked up at him and blushed all over. She had never seen a naked man in the flesh before, didn't know that this was how a man would look when he was aroused. She became a little frightened, but terribly excited, too. This was what her body was made for, and it was on fire with a primitive, urgent need to be taken. She reached up for him. 'Rhys. Oh, Rhys, I love you so much. I want you so much.'

His breathing was harsh in his throat, bending over her he ran his hand down her body, felt the great quiver of mingled excitement and trepidation that ran through her. Lifting his eyes, Rhys read the nervous apprehension in hers. Suddenly he drew back, hesitated, then stood up. Going into the bathroom he put on a robe, came back and sat on the edge of the bed. Because he had clothes on, Alix immediately felt embarrassed at being naked. Pulling the quilt up around her, she looked at him uncertainly.

His eyes studying her face, Rhys said, 'Alix, are you on the Pill?'

The flush deepened and she shook her head.

He sighed. 'I thought not. You expected me, then, to take any precautions necessary?'

'Well . . . yes.'

'Didn't it occur to you that I might not have anything? I didn't expect this, and I'm not in the habit of sleeping with other women; so why should you expect it?'

Alix's fingers tightened on the quilt and she looked away. Bitterness and disappointment filled her heart because she knew that she'd failed; the hunger had gone from Rhys's eyes and she knew he wouldn't make love to her now.

'Well?' Rhys said compellingly.

'I don't know. I didn't—I didn't think about that side of it.'

His eyebrows rose and there was a distinctly chill note in his voice as Rhys said, 'Hardly a responsible attitude.'

'We've been engaged for over a year,' she burst out. 'We're in love, for heaven's sake—or supposed to be. Why shouldn't we go to bed together without—without being clinical about it? Why don't we go to bed together at all, if it comes to that?'

Reaching out, Rhys went to put his arms round her, but Alix was so upset that for the first time in her life she shook him off. Taking no notice, Rhys took hold of her and made her look at him. 'I thought we agreed that we would do this properly,' he said soothingly as she began to cry. 'Have a white wedding and a honeymoon that *is* a honeymoon, not be like so many other couples and already know everything there is to know about one another.'

'I didn't agree it, it was what you said. And why shouldn't we go to bed together first? We might find that we're incompatible.'

To her annoyance Rhys burst into laughter. 'Us? Incompatible? You're joking.' And he hugged her, still laughing.

Alix had to smile, albeit reluctantly. 'You wanted me just now.'

'Of course I did. You're beautiful. Beautiful enough to undermine all my good intentions.'

'Not quite,' she said with regret.

Rhys's face sobered. 'Do you really want our first time to be like this? Is this what you want to look back on; a mere hasty sexual encounter? Or a wedding night when we have all the time in the world to make love, tenderly, slowly, savouring every moment?'

Put like that, there was only one answer she could make, but Alix wasn't sure that she wouldn't rather have had it like this, an act of spontaneity and passionate hunger, something that neither of them could resist. 'Yes, I'd like that,' she agreed.

'Well, we have plenty of time to——'

'No, we don't!' she broke in angrily. 'I'm sick to death of you saying we have plenty of time.' Raising her eyes she met his. 'I want it soon, Rhys.'

He gave a thin smile. 'That sounds ominously like a threat.' She didn't speak, just held his eyes, and he gave a shrug. 'All right, urchin, you win. Go ahead and set a date—but just make sure it's at a time when I have a few weeks free.'

CHAPTER FOUR

ALIX had scored a victory and ought to have been jubilant, but strangely didn't feel that way. The dinner party wasn't very successful; Todd and his wife, Lynette, appeared to have had a row earlier and she wasn't doing a very good job of concealing it. She was sitting between Rhys and the other male guest and almost ignored Todd, instead openly flirting with Rhys. Alix, who was seated opposite, between Todd and the other man, was getting angrier by the minute, especially when Rhys made no attempt to rebuff Lynette and even danced with her and the other woman guest before he danced with Alix.

If Lynette hadn't been the boss's wife, Alix would have made a 'keep off, this man is mine' comment, but she had to just sit there and smile, which nearly killed her.

When they got in the car she was angrier with Rhys than she'd ever been before.

'I'll drive you back to Kent,' he told her.

'Don't bother; I can take a train,' she answered stiffly.

Rhys glanced at her, saw the mutinous set of her mouth. 'Alix, you know I can't stand women who sulk, so just——'

'Then you shouldn't have given me cause!' she interrupted fiercely. 'How dare you flirt with that ghastly woman?'

Rhys's jaw hardened. 'I wasn't flirting with her.'

'But you certainly weren't stopping her from flirting with *you*. You even danced with her before me!'

77

'So that's what rankles, is it? If you were listening you would have heard her ask me for that dance because the tune was one of her favourites, and Todd wasn't in the mood for dancing.'

'No, because they'd had a row. Couldn't you see that she was just using you because of it?'

'No woman *uses* me, Alix—not even you,' Rhys said shortly.

'Is that why you did it, then; because I'd pushed you into finally setting a date?'

He didn't openly admit it, but said, 'I don't like being coerced.'

'Oh, really? Has it ever occurred to you that that's exactly what you've been doing to me for the last eighteen months?'

'Don't be ridiculous,' Rhys said tersely. 'I always said that we'd get married once I took over from Todd. And what the hell is there to argue about anyway? You've got what you want. I've agreed to get married now even though I'll still have to be away a lot and we won't have the settled life that I wanted, that I've been working for.'

Rhys had the power to make her feel guilty, and she felt that way now. After all it wasn't his fault that Todd had to stay in England for another year; it was that damn Lynette's. Alix felt a profound hatred for the woman who had delayed her marriage, who had caused her to coerce Rhys, who had even dared to flirt with him right in front of her. She put the hatred aside, but stored it in her mind.

But pride made her say stiffly, 'I'm sorry. If you don't want to get married now you don't have to. You don't have to marry me *at all* if you don't want to.'

'Of course I want to marry you.'

'Really? I'm beginning to wonder.'

'Don't be so damn childish.'

'I am not a child!' she declared angrily, sitting forward in her seat, her body tense.

Rhys swore under his breath. 'Do we have to argue about this while I'm driving?'

'Stop, then. Let me drive.'

To her surprise, Rhys did pull in to the side of the road. She went to open her door, to go round to the driver's side, but Rhys reached out and pulled her roughly to him. 'There's only one way to deal with an argumentative chit like you,' he said tersely, and put a hand behind her head as he took her mouth.

For a few moments she resisted him, tried to turn away, but his grip tightened and she had no alternative but to let him do what he wanted. Soon his kiss, as always, aroused her senses. Alix gave a small sigh and, abandoning the vain struggle, surrendered her lips to him. Her arms went round his neck and she was lost in the welcome forgetfulness of everything else except being in his arms.

'Idiot,' Rhys breathed against her neck when he at last released her lips. 'Don't ever say that to me again. Not want to marry you, indeed! You know you're the only girl in the world I want.'

'Oh, Rhys,' Alix gave him a misty-eyed look. 'We've had our first real fight.'

He gave a burst of laughter, but then grinned at her teasingly. 'Let's do it again—I'm enjoying making up.'

She gave a shudder. 'No, definitely not. I don't like it at all.'

'OK, we won't.' Rhys put a finger to trace the outline of her lips, saw the questioning look in her eyes and said on a rather rueful note, 'Yes, you can go ahead and set the wedding date. I've got parents and grandparents ganging up on me as it is; I can't hold out against you as well.'

She gave him a troubled look. 'Is it so bad, wanting to be married soon?' And added, with difficulty, 'I'm—I'm nearly twenty-two, Rhys. I'm ready to be married or—or loved.'

His eyes were on her face, but his was in shadow and she couldn't read his reaction. His finger grew still as he gazed down at her. 'Yes, I suppose you are,' he agreed on an odd note. 'My little urchin, waking up to sensuality.'

'You've made me feel like that. The way you kiss me... What you do to me. But it isn't enough any more.'

Rhys made a small sound that was suspiciously like a sigh. 'No, I suppose I should have seen that. Can you last out until this wedding is arranged?'

She smiled. 'I might make it.'

'Good.' He kissed her lightly. 'In that case——'

He broke off as someone rapped on the window, and turned to see a policeman standing by the car. Quickly Rhys lowered the window.

'Do you know you're parked on a double yellow line, sir?'

Rhys rose to the occasion magnificently. 'I'm so sorry, Constable. You see, this lady has agreed to marry me, and I just had to stop and—er—show her how pleased I am.'

'Just got engaged, have you?' The policeman's tone immediately softened. 'Well, congratulations—but you'll have to let her know how you feel somewhere that doesn't have a yellow line.'

'Yes, Constable. Thank you. We'll move on at once.'

They managed to contain their laughter until they'd driven away, and for a while Alix felt happy again because she was young enough to think that quarrelling and making up afterwards was romantic. It was only when Rhys dropped her at her house and she lay in bed, going over the evening, that she realised that even though she'd got what she wanted, most of it had turned out to be a mess. She had made Rhys angry, which she'd never done before, and that made her feel terrible—guilty and unhappy. And she'd never actually hated anyone before, her own warm friendliness always having produced the same reaction in others, but now she found that her dislike of Lynette Weston couldn't be dispelled. It was her fault that she had quarrelled with Rhys, and Alix found that she couldn't forgive her for it.

She was still feeling low the next morning, but when she told her mother that Rhys had agreed to set a date her mother was over the moon. 'Oh, thank goodness for that! I've already bought three wedding outfits and I thought I'd have to buy yet another because the styles have changed again. Did he say when, dear?'

'No, just said arrange it when we liked but to make sure he was free at work.'

'And when do you think that will be?'

'I don't know. I'll have to have a look at his schedule when I go into work on Monday. Not for a couple of months at least, I shouldn't think.'

'Well, even that isn't very long when you're preparing a wedding. It will be difficult to hire a hotel at short notice; we'll probably have to have a marquee in the garden. I'd better phone Joanne and ask her what she thinks.'

Alix left the two mothers talking on the phone and wandered out into the garden. Her father had put stepping-stones in the lawn leading up to the gate in the hedge, at first for her benefit, but they all used them now, going back and forth between the two houses, as close as any people who were not related could be, closer perhaps. Usually when Rhys was home Alix would run through the gate to find him, but today she lingered in her own garden, within sight of his bedroom window, sitting on the old swing, idly pushing herself back and forth.

The gate latch clicked and Alix looked round eagerly, but it was Aunt Joanne.

'Isn't this wonderful?' Rhys's mother said with a beaming smile. 'I'm so glad we can go ahead with the wedding. I've come to discuss plans with you and your mother.'

'Isn't Rhys coming?'

'No, he's gone sailing with David and your father.' She must have noticed the disappointment in Alix's face, because she took her hand and said, 'Men are really a great nuisance when it comes to weddings, Alix. They're much better out of the way. All they do is want to invite old school chums they haven't seen or heard from for the last thirty years, or else grumble about the cost. So long as they turn up at the church on time and wearing the right clothes, then we're better off without them.'

She linked arms with Alix and they walked down to the house, where Alix's mother was waiting. She said much the same thing, adding that men weren't really interested in weddings and couldn't wait to escape from all the preparations. So the three of them settled down to talk bridesmaids and dresses, found the guest list they'd originally made over eighteen months ago and brought it up to date. Ordinarily Alix would have loved it all, but she was still troubled about last night, and had wanted to see Rhys to reassure herself that all was well between them. Ideally, she would have liked to go sailing with him herself, just the two of them of course, and had more than expected him to suggest it.

With an inner sigh, she gave her attention instead to the wedding plans, although she found that her heart wasn't in that, either. To Alix, their wedding-day would be the climax to the one ambition of her life, and she had wanted Rhys to share it all; it wasn't very pleasant to think that he had gone out sailing, had 'escaped', rather than come and join in the discussions. After a while she said, rather impatiently, 'It's pointless making all these plans when we don't have a date yet. I'll phone you from work on Monday with some dates and then you can decide where to hold the reception.' She stood up. 'Excuse me. I think I'll go into Canterbury and do some shopping.'

'For a going-away outfit? Won't you have a better chance of something stylish in London, dear,' Aunt Joanne suggested.

'Yes, probably—but I think I'll go anyway.'

Canterbury was only twenty minutes way, but it took another twenty to queue for the car park; Saturday was always a busy day in the town, and, as it was so near the Channel coast, there were lots of French people over for the day, swelling the crowds. Alix wandered round the shopping precinct for a while, then went through the old stone arch, across the cathedral close, and into the huge, ancient building. There were tourists here, too, being taken round by the guides, but she found a seat in a quiet corner and looked down at the choir stalls leading to the high altar. It was here that she was to be married, if it could be arranged. And it most probably would be, as permission had been given to her father ages ago.

Alix had been here before to imagine what it would be like, had sat in blissful happiness as she pictured becoming Rhys's wife at last. But today she couldn't get back into that state of euphoric happiness no matter how hard she tried. She wished now that she had never given Rhys that ultimatum, because that, really, was what it had been. But she wished, even more, that she hadn't been driven to it. Reality had started to creep into her dream, and Alix dimly saw that the rosiness of it had paled a little.

She sat there for some while longer, then went out into the town and rang her mother to say that she wouldn't be home to dinner.

'Are you all right, Alix?' her mother asked on a concerned note.

'Yes, of course. I've run into a couple of old school friends and we're going to have a meal and then go on to a film or something. Don't wait up for me.'

'No, dear. Have a good time.'

But Alix might have known that her mother wouldn't obey her; she was in the sitting-room, watching television, when Alix quietly let herself into the house around midnight.

'I'm in here, dear.'

Alix put her head round the door, hoping to say a brief goodnight, but her mother beckoned her in.

'What film did you see?'

Alix told her, truthfully, but had to lie about the imaginary friends.

Her mother gave her an intent look, but didn't pursue it, instead saying, 'Alix, is there something you want to tell me?'

'Not that I can think of,' Alix answered as casually as she could. 'Mum, I'm really tired. I think I'll——'

But, 'Something that you *ought* to tell me, then?' her mother pursued.

Alix flushed, guessing what her mother was driving at. 'I've already said no.'

Taking her hand, the older woman looked at her earnestly and said, 'You and Rhys have been engaged for quite some time now; it wouldn't be at all surprising if you'd—made a mistake. Is that why you've decided to set a date now? Why you don't seem so happy about it?'

Her face scarlet, Alix stood up. 'No, it isn't.' Adding on a burst of anger. 'It would be a bit difficult to have made a mistake when we've never once made love!' And she turned and ran out of the room, leaving her mother staring after her.

Afterwards, lying in her bed, Alix remembered the look of astonishment on her mother's face, and thought rather indignantly that she would have been less shocked if she'd announced that she was pregnant! It took a moment for the contrariness of the idea to sink in, then Alix chuckled in amusement. Her parents had been the teenagers of the sixties and in some ways were far more broad-minded than her own generation. She had certainly been astounded to learn that she and Rhys had never made love; so was Alix, if it came to that.

Next day, Sunday, Alix and her parents had to go into Hampshire to visit an aunt, who was recovering from an operation. They had lunch on the way back, then

visited a craft fair, because her mother was into that kind
of thing, so it was quite late when they got home. It was
Rhys's last day at home, he had to go to Prague the next
morning and expected to be away for at least a couple
of weeks. Normally Alix would have gone round to his
place to see him, but things weren't normal and he had
gone sailing without a word yesterday. So she decided
to wait and let him make the first move.

After going up to her room to change, Alix lay on her
bed, the CD player on low, reading a book, but listening
for the phone. No call came but around nine o'clock
there was a whistle outside her window. Quickly she
opened it and saw Rhys standing below.

'Are you going to stay there all night or are you coming
for a walk?' he demanded.

She had decided to play hard to get, but at sight of
him all her resolution vanished. 'I'll be right down.'
Grabbing up a jacket, she ran out to join him.

Putting his arms round her, Rhys kissed her. 'Had a
good day?'

'It was OK.' He let her go and they began to walk
down towards the meadow. 'How about you?'

'I helped my father repair the roof of the garage.'

'And yesterday, when you went sailing?'

Rhys glanced at her, alerted by her tone. 'The sailing
was great, but it turned out that our two fathers had got
hold of me for a business talk.'

'Why, what happened?'

'We moored off a buoy to have our picnic lunch and
they started talking money.'

'To pay for the wedding, do you mean?'

'Partly that. My father has decided to retire early. He
was asking your father for advice.'

As her father was a financial consultant, this was hardly surprising. But Alix said, 'He could ask my father's advice any time. Why when you were out sailing, and why when you were there?'

'Good question. You know some years ago they bought that piece of ground at the end of our gardens? Well, they wanted to know how I'd feel if they gave it to us for a wedding present.'

'A piece of ground?'

'To build a house on. For us to live in.'

'Oh, I see.' They had reached the fence and Alix stopped and looked at him. 'What did you say?'

'I said that it was very kind of them.'

There was an ironic note to his voice that made her study him more intently, to wish that it was daylight. 'Was that a yes or a no?'

He shrugged non-committally. 'If you want a house there, we'll build one.'

But there had been no great enthusiasm in his tone and she had to feel her way as she said, 'I suppose, from their point of view, it would have great advantages. We would be near at hand, for when they get older. And they would be able, hopefully, to see their grandchildren all the time.' He made no comment so she went on, making her voice light, 'And I suppose it would be an asset for us—built-in baby-sitters.'

'I'll tell them that we accept, then.'

She caught his hand. 'No! Not unless you want it, too,' she said forcefully. 'I don't want you to feel— coerced again. I don't care where I live so long as it's with you.'

'Thanks, urchin.' Putting his finger under her chin, Rhys tilted her face towards him. 'I must admit that I've felt as if everyone is ganging up on me lately.' His lips teased hers, touching them too lightly for it to be called a kiss. 'But you shall have your house, urchin. Whatever you want to make you happy. Only I'm afraid you'll have to wait for a while; I won't be here long enough to oversee it being built for quite some time.'

'Unless your father does it for you,' Alix said without thinking. 'If he's going to retire he'll be here all the time.'

Immediately she sensed a withdrawal in him. 'Now, why didn't I think of that?' he said shortly.

'Because it was a stupid thing to say,' she said at once, cursing herself for a fool. 'Of course you want to make sure the house is just as we want it.'

But it was too late. Rhys straightened and said, 'No, it will give Dad something to do. He'll enjoy it. And you and mother, and your parents, will all be able to help him. It's a great idea. Saves me a good deal of bother.'

'Rhys, please. I'm sorry. I——' She broke off as he turned away.

'We'd better get back. I have to be at the airport at some ungodly hour in the morning.'

'I'll drive you.'

'There's no point. I'm only going from Gatwick. I'll drive myself and leave the car in the car park.'

'Please, I want to.'

But he refused, and although he kissed her when he said goodnight Alix lay awake that night, worrying that things weren't right between them again. She dropped off to sleep eventually but woke when her alarm clock went off at four. She dressed in the dark, then sat by her window, looking across the garden to Rhys's bedroom, waiting for the light to come on. When it went out again, half an hour later, she ran downstairs and let herself out. Ran across the garden to wait by his garage until Rhys came out to the car.

He started with surprise when he saw her, but she didn't wait for him to say anything before throwing herself into his arms. 'Rhys, please don't be angry with me. I love you so much. We'll do whatever you want, whatever you say.' She looked up at him, her eyes full of entreaty. 'Please don't leave feeling angry with me.'

Dropping his case, Rhys put his arms round her. 'I'm not angry with you, urchin.' He looked rueful. 'Events seem to be overtaking me, that's all. I was hoping that we'd be able to do things in our own time, but it seems that I have less of it than anyone else. But I'm not angry, really. Just a bit disappointed that I won't be here to share it all. But you'll manage fine without me. Just send me lots of faxes, telling me what you're up to.' Suddenly fierce, he bent to kiss her. 'And maybe it's just as well we're getting married soon,' he said on a husky note. 'Because I'm not sure how much longer I can hold out.'

It was what she wanted to hear, exactly the right words. When Rhys let her go Alix was breathless, her eyes sparkling happily. 'Oh, Rhys, I *do* love you,' she said in deep sincerity as he got in the car.

He grinned at her, one of the lazy grins that she adored. 'See you in a couple of weeks. Take care, urchin.' And he waved as he drove away.

Alix rushed into work the next morning and went into Todd's office to look at the work schedules. Apart from an odd week here and there, Rhys looked to be booked up for at least the next five months. She was standing before the planning chart, looking up at it disconsolately, when Todd came in. He put a hand on her drooping shoulder.

'Hi, Alix. What's so interesting?'

'I was trying to find two or three clear weeks so Rhys and I can get married,' she told him. 'But there's nothing for months.'

'You've decided not to wait any longer, have you? Well, I certainly don't blame Rhys for that. And getting married is pretty important. So important in fact——' he picked up the pen that hung by the chart '—that I think we might just make one or two alterations. Let's see, now... June is a pretty good month for a wedding, isn't it? So if we get someone to take over from Rhys on this Lithuanian project, then that will give him nearly a month's leave starting at the beginning of June. That's just over two months from now. That suit you, Alix?'

'That's just—just fantastic!' She turned to him, elation in her blue eyes. 'Thanks, Todd. It means so much to me.'

'Anything for my favourite PA.' Putting his arm round her waist, Todd gave her a friendly hug. 'Mind you, I shall expect an invitation to the wedding.'

'You and Lynette will be the guests of honour,' Alix assured him.

A shadow dulled his smile. 'I hope it will be the two of us, but it might be just me, honey; Lynette and I are having a few problems right now.'

'Oh, Todd, I'm sorry to hear that. Not serious, I hope?'

He shrugged. 'We'll just have to wait and see.'

Alix felt genuine sympathy for Todd, because she knew that he loved his family, especially his sons, but she had none for Lynette, whom she blamed for creating Todd's problems, and whom she had begun to think of as a first-class bitch.

Going back to her own office, Alix immediately put through a fax to the hotel in Prague where Rhys was staying, telling him the good news, then rang her mother and told her.

'That's marvellous, dear,' Mrs North enthused. 'Now, what date shall we pick?'

'I'm not sure. I haven't actually spoken to Rhys about it.'

'Well, he will probably want to be home for a few days before the wedding, so I think we'll make it the tenth of June. That will give you three whole weeks for your honeymoon.'

'That sounds fine, but perhaps I ought to check with Rhys first.'

'Oh, I don't think so, dear. He told you to go ahead and fix it, didn't he?'

'Well, yes, but——'

'That's all right, then. We'll work on that date.'

Alix agreed, but, when she'd put the phone down, wished that she'd been a bit firmer about getting Rhys's agreement first; but her mother was right, he had told her to go ahead and just keep him informed by fax. Anyway, he was bound to phone her either at work or at the flat tonight, and if he had any reservations he could tell her then. To be on the safe side, Alix sent him another fax. 'Chosen June tenth for big day. OK with you?'

But he didn't phone, and it was three days before he answered by sending a fax to the office, and then it was just three words. 'June tenth OK.'

Alix had rushed eagerly to tear the sheet off the machine, but then stood looking at it with mixed emotions. Rhys must have thought that someone else might read it, and that's why he hadn't sent his love or anything. But these terse words were hardly those of a lover, of a man eager to claim her for his own at last. But at least he'd agreed; she didn't have to worry any longer that he might not.

Feeling strangely low, Alix went downstairs to find Kathy. They were still firm friends, although Kathy was already married, the result of a whirlwind courtship after meeting her future husband by nearly knocking him out with a badly hit tennis ball a year ago. 'He fell in love with me the moment he recovered consciousness,' as Kathy liked to joke.

'Hello, Kathy. Doing anything for lunch?'

'Oh, sorry, Alix. I have to do some shopping. Our best man and his new girlfriend are coming to dinner.' She gave Alix an appraising look. 'Anything the matter?'

'No. Are you and that husband of yours doing anything on the tenth of June?'

Kathy fished a diary out of her bag. 'Tenth of June? No, we're free. Why, what's happ——' She broke off, her mouth falling open. 'Alix! You don't mean you've finally set a date?'

Alix nodded, grinning, and immediately feeling better.

'That's wonderful! Of course we're free. I wouldn't miss your wedding for anything.'

Alix was greatly touched because, although she had gone to Kathy's wedding, Rhys had been away. The wedding had been fun, but not nearly as much as it would have been if Rhys had been with her. She was so proud of him, so loved to show him off, and always had her morale lifted a million times when she was with him.

They had a chat about a wedding-dress and going-away outfit for a few minutes, and met up in the cloakroom later for a longer chat, all of which made Alix feel great again, and to dismiss her earlier feeling of restlessness as nerves.

By the time Rhys was due home again, Alix was not only her usual happy self, but full of excitement over the wedding plans which were going ahead at a fast pace back home in Kent. The cathedral and a hotel for the reception had been definitely booked, bridesmaids and pages had been told to stand by to be measured for their outfits, and Alix had chosen the dress she wanted. A friend of her mother's had promised to make the cake, and a florist had been engaged for the flowers. Now that they had finally set the date, their two mothers had gone to work like a programmed machine that had just been waiting to be switched on, and everything was happening efficiently and fast. Alix was consulted at every stage, of course, but found that she had little to do except say yes.

The trip to Prague was a comparatively short one, just to finalise some details and sign the contract, so Rhys was soon home. He seemed his usual self, and content with all the wedding arrangements that bombarded him from all sides as soon as he arrived. But he was only in Kent for a day or so before going off to spend the week sailing round the Scottish Isles with friends. As he explained to Alix before he left, 'It will probably be my last chance to have a holiday like this.'

'I don't see why,' she protested.

'After we're married we'll presumably be spending all our free time together. I'll look on this as my last bachelor holiday,' he added with a rueful grin.

He said it lightly enough, but Alix didn't like the ruefulness, and couldn't help but think that he was reluctant to give up his sailing holidays, even to spend the time with her. She felt guilty about it and determined, once they were married, to make sure he kept up his friendships and did his own thing whenever he wanted. She didn't want to be the kind of wife that kept her husband at her side the whole time; although, for herself, she could never contemplate going away with girlfriends when she could be with Rhys. But everyone knew that men were different; her own father liked to go on golfing holidays with his friends, Rhys's father included. But her mother cheerfully said that Rhys was just escaping from all the fuss of the wedding.

When he returned he came into the office to see Todd. Alix was in her own, outer office, and stayed there; she always tried to maintain a professional manner towards Todd and Rhys in the office, never butting in on them when they were talking business, or taking advantage of her relationship with Rhys. So when Todd's buzzer sounded it was Brenda who went in to see him. But she left the door ajar and Alix, her ears attuned to Rhys's voice, heard him say angrily, 'Damn it, Todd, you should have consulted me before you took me off that project. It will be a great advantage for us to get a foothold there. And there's so much competition for the market that——'

Brenda came back and shut the door, but Alix had heard enough to guess that Rhys was talking about the Lithuanian project. The one he would have gone on if

Todd hadn't changed it to give him time to get married. It hurt a little, but she knew by now that his work was extremely important to Rhys; maybe he would have preferred a different time but it was too late now; the date was set and everything going ahead.

He left again the next day, for New Zealand this time, taking a team to work out a tender for a new airport, and wasn't expected back for a month. His mother made sure she had his measurements for his morning suit, the name of the best man and the list of friends he wanted to act as ushers; apart from that there seemed little for him to do.

At times the month he was away dragged, at others it flew by. Todd was mostly in England, trying desperately to patch up his marriage, but his wife was English and had been too long in England to want to go back to Canada to live. She and her sons had all their friends here, as she pointed out. But Todd was Canadian through and through and wanted his sons to be brought up there as well as in England, so that they, too, would know and love the country. But if didn't seem as if this was their only problem; Alix had heard a whisper that Lynette was seeing someone else. Alix didn't want to believe it for Todd's sake, but several times, when she went into his office, she found him seated at his desk, gazing broodingly into space, which was totally unlike him.

Alix duly sent them a joint invitation to the wedding, but although Todd accepted at once, he said he wasn't sure about Lynette. 'She's thinking of taking a trip to France; I'm not sure she'll be back in time.'

'Why don't you go with her?' Alix suggested. 'You need a break.'

But he only shrugged and said, 'I may have to go to Lithuania in Rhys's place. Depends how it goes.'

When Rhys came back from New Zealand Alix hardly saw him. He disappeared into his own office with his team and worked intensely on the tender for the airport. There was only three weeks to the wedding, so Alix naturally thought that he was working so hard in order to get the job finished before then. She moved out of the flat, as she always did when he came home, happily thinking that when next she lived there it would be as Rhys's wife. Rhys came down to Kent for the first weekend, but spent it trying on his suit, buying presents for the bridesmaids, fixing up their honeymoon, so that Alix didn't see much of him then, either. And she herself was busy, deciding on what flowers she wanted, going with the two mothers to the cathedral to see what floral decorations would be needed there, then going to the hotel to decide on a menu; the arrangements seemed to be endless. Alix was more than grateful that their two mothers were such close friends and agreed on everything; if there had been arguments in which she would have had to intervene, life would have been hell. But as it was, everyone was working hard to make the day absolutely perfect for her.

At home everything was fine. It was at the office that it all started to go wrong. Rhys finished the New Zealand tender in record time, then calmly told her that he was going to Lithuania.

'What?' Alix stared at him in consternation.

'Don't worry. I'll be back in plenty of time for the tenth.'

'But I thought you were rushing the New Zealand job through so that you'd be free to make the most of getting ready for the wedding.'

'Make the most of it?' He raised an eyebrow.

'You only get married once,' Alix pointed out rather tartly. 'Why shouldn't you enjoy the preparations?'

They were alone in her office. Rhys bent to kiss her lightly. 'You enjoy it for me. Seriously, urchin, I'll feel a whole lot happier if I can go to Vilnius, size up the situation and speak to our contacts there before the team goes in. It will only take a few days. And you would much rather I was relaxed and unworried on our honeymoon, now wouldn't you?'

Alix was quite sure he would be relaxed, she'd see to that; but, knowing there was no other course, she dutifully said, 'I suppose so. But there are still lots of things you're needed for, Rhys.'

'I've briefed my father; he'll take care of anything urgent that crops up, and I'll deal with the rest when I get back.' Leaning forward, he spread his hands on the desk and leaned over it to kiss her properly.

'Hey! Put that girl down! She's still mine in working hours. You can't have her until after five-thirty,' Todd exclaimed, walking in on them.

'Don't you knock?' Rhys complained, straightening up.

'I shouldn't have to. Put a sign on the door if you can't keep your hands off her.'

Alix laughed, loving the banter between them, not unpleased at being caught. Todd took Rhys away with him and she only saw him again briefly when he came to say goodbye. They were alone then, too, and she clung to him, not wanting him to go.

'I'll soon be back,' he told her. Putting his hands low on her hips, he drew her against him, moved, and watched her eyes darken as desire took hold. He smiled then, and leaning forward, whispered outrageously in her ear, 'Keep it hot for me, urchin.'

Her face flamed, making him laugh, but then the phone rang to say that his car was ready, so he said goodbye and left.

The next thing to go wrong at the office was caused by Todd's wife. Lynette came unexpectedly to the office to see him. Ordinarily Alix would have interrupted Todd, whatever he was doing, and shown her right in, but remembering the rumours and knowing what a hard time she'd been giving her boss lately, Alix told Lynette he was busy and made her wait. Lynette went off to the ladies' cloakroom, came back in ten minutes, but again Alix said that Todd couldn't be interrupted. After pacing the floor in growing anger for another ten minutes, Lynette just stormed into his room, where Todd was merely talking on the phone.

'Did you tell Alix to keep me out?' Alix heard her demanding of him furiously.

The door slammed and she didn't hear any more, not specific words, that was; but she certainly heard their raised voices as the two had a real, stand-up fight. Soon, Lynette slammed her way out of Todd's room again and would have marched out of the building, but she noticed Alix and changed her mind, coming striding over to her.

'I won't be coming to your wedding,' she announced shortly.

'Oh, won't you?' Alix tried hard to look disappointed.

'No—because the whole affair is just a travesty anyway.'

Alix frowned in puzzlement. 'A travesty?'

'Yes.' Lynette gave her a contemptuous look. 'You stupid little idiot. Why do you think Rhys has put off your marriage as long as he possibly could? He doesn't care about you. The only reason he's getting married at all is because it was a condition of taking over from Todd. The company insisted on him being married if he wanted the job. He had to get married so he chose you, someone he could keep putting off until he had to, keep delaying the wedding until he actually took over Todd's job.' She laughed. 'You look like a fish standing there with your mouth open! If you don't believe me, ask Rhys yourself. He doesn't love you. He never has and he never will. You're just the silly chit who's always adored him and will always let him do what he wants!' She laughed again, then turned and strode triumphantly out of the room.

CHAPTER FIVE

ALIX didn't ask Rhys; she asked Todd instead. But not immediately. Her first reaction was that Lynette's outburst had just been rubbish, made up on the spur of the moment by a vindictive mind, because she'd been kept waiting. And because she'd rowed with Todd, of course; Alix wasn't at all surprised that Lynette had taken it out on her; she'd always thought she was that kind of woman.

At first she sat in her chair feeling stunned, the way one did when confronted by unwarranted and unexpected rudeness, but then, insidiously, a whole lot of questions began to arise in her mind. Was it really true that Rhys needed to be married to take over the English branch of the company? The idea wasn't as archaic as it sounded; Todd's father had been a great man for traditional values, and he might easily have laid down that rule, feeling that family men were more stable, more likely to stay in the job and not get into trouble when abroad. But was it still part of company policy now, in this more advanced age? If it was, then a whole lot of disturbing facts seemed to fit. It was undeniably true that Rhys had said they would be married when he took over from Todd. Try as she might, Alix couldn't wriggle out of that one. And it was also true that when Todd's transfer to Canada was delayed Rhys took it that the wedding would also be delayed, and would have put it off for yet another year if she hadn't brought things to a head and demanded they set a date.

With those unwelcome thoughts in her mind, Alix had to try to face up to the other taunt that Lynette had thrown at her: that Rhys didn't love her. But heart took over from head with that one. *No way*! Everything screamed out a rejection. Of course he loved her! If he had to have a wife, then Rhys could pick any girl he chose. He was so good-looking and attractive to women that they were always throwing themselves at him. Why, Alix remembered once when they'd gone out to dinner at a restaurant and she'd gone to the cloakroom for five minutes. When she came back she found some girl, a total stranger, had actually come across to the table to talk to him. And had the audacity to give him her phone number, too! Rhys had laughed when Alix had been indignant and said, 'Don't worry, urchin, I don't look at other women when I'm with you.'

But that memory was disturbing, too. At the time she had been completely happy with it, but now, because of that rotten Lynette, even that reassurance sounded ambiguous.

Alix pushed it out of her mind. Rhys loved her. Maybe not as much as she loved him, and certainly not for as long, but he definitely loved her. He'd told her so. Not often. But he had told her. Alix's thoughts went back to that precious night when they'd walked down to the meadow, soon after they'd become officially engaged. Rhys had kissed her then, and told her he loved her because of her innocence. But that wasn't quite right. She frowned, concentrating, dusting off the memory. No, what he'd actually said was that her innocence was what he loved about her. The same thing, then? Or was it?

Before Lynette's outburst Alix would never have questioned it, but now it sent her hurrying into Todd's office without even knocking at the door.

'Is it true?' she demanded coming up to his desk.

He looked up in surprise from where he'd been sitting with his head in his hands. 'Huh?'

'Is it true that Rhys can't take over your job from you unless he's married?'

'What?' Todd frowned, straightened, then looked into her face, pale, and sharpened by tension. 'What put that idea into your head?'

There was a slight wariness in his voice but Alix was too strung up to notice. 'Your wife. Lynette. She told me. She said that——'

Lifting a hand to stop her, Todd rose and came round his desk to put a reassuring hand on her shoulder. 'Alix, honey, I'm really sorry. I'm afraid Lyn and I had a real humdinger of a fight just now. She went out in a hell of a temper and I'm afraid you got in the way. If Brenda had been in the office she would probably have had a go at her instead. I'm sorry, you shouldn't have to be involved in this. But—well, I guess you know, things have been getting worse between us lately.'

'I guessed,' Alix admitted. 'But——'

'I think it's going to come down to a court case for possession of the kids,' Todd went on. 'I've been trying everything I know to try and avoid that, but Lyn won't go to Canada and she won't even compromise.'

'I'm very sorry,' Alix said. 'I really am. But, Todd—is it true?'

'Is what true? Oh, you mean about Rhys. Hell, Alix, he's the best man for the job. You know that. Anybody who works as hard as he does for the company deserves it.'

'Yes, but——'

'Do you really think I wouldn't have given him the job just because he wasn't married?' Todd went on. 'This is business, Alix. You have to be practical.' He shook his head, went over to the cabinet and poured himself a drink, a stiff one, Alix noticed. 'You want a drink, kid? You look as if you could do with one.'

She nodded, suddenly feeling weak and shaken, and sank down into one of Todd's deep leather armchairs. 'She shouldn't have said that,' she said tremulously. 'All those things.'

'What things?' Todd came over and put the glass in her hand, took a good slug of his.

Remembering that Todd and Lynette were still married and that, presumably, he still loved her, Alix said, 'It—it doesn't matter.'

Todd sighed. 'You might as well tell me, Alix. What other poison has she been spreading?'

Painfully, finding it hard to even say the words, Alix said, 'She told me that Rhys didn't love me. That he never had.'

Todd burst into laughter. 'Can you beat that? Well, that proves that Lyn was so angry she just said the first things that came into her head. Everyone knows the guy's nuts about you. Why, he bores the pants off people, the way he never stops talking about you.'

'Really?' Alix lifted glowing eyes to meet his.

'Sure. But you know that; I don't have to tell you.'

She smiled. 'Yes, of course. It just came as rather a shock to be told, just a few days before your wedding, that the bridegroom doesn't love you.'

Todd nodded in rueful admiration. 'I have to give it to Lynette; she really knows how to hit you where it hurts.'

'But she fights dirty,' Alix pointed out wryly.

'Yeah.'

They sat and sipped their drinks, both looking gloomy, both with their thoughts on the same woman. Alix didn't know what Todd was thinking, but hers were full of bitterness and hate. She felt physically and mentally shaken by what had happened. How could anyone be so cruel? What real harm had she ever done to Lynette, for heaven's sake? But the woman had openly flirted with Rhys and then had the nerve to turn round and say with absolute certainty that he didn't love her, Alix. While all the time Lynette herself was having an affair with some unknown man! For the briefest of seconds a cold finger of dread entered Alix's heart but was instantly dismissed—no, not dismissed, wasn't allowed to even take hold.

Finishing the drink in one mind-numbing swallow, she set the glass down and said jerkily, 'It's my hen party tonight.'

'Yeah, I heard. Quite a few of the girls are going, aren't they?'

'Yes.'

'Here.' Todd fumbled some money from his wallet. 'Buy them all a drink on me.'

'Thank you.' Alix looked at the notes without really taking them in, but said automatically, 'That's far too much.'

'Are you staying in London tonight?'

'Yes.'

'Then get drunk. Forget about Lynette.'

She laughed rather shakily. 'I just might do that. It should be a good night.'

'I hope so. It's a pity Rhys isn't going to make it back for his party. Still, we'll all——'

'*What* did you say?' Alix broke in.

Todd slowly lifted his eyes to look at her. 'You—haven't heard yet?'

'No, I haven't heard anything,' she said curtly. 'Is it true? Rhys is actually not coming home for his stag party?' Her voice rose in indignant anger.

'It seems that a small hiccup had cropped up in Lithuania. Something he feels he has to deal with. I thought he must have spoken to you about it when he rang this morning.'

'No. He didn't,' Alix said shortly.

'The line was real bad. Maybe he got cut off. Or maybe he thought he'd tell you when he rings tonight.'

Her chin lifted. 'Yes, I expect that's what he means to do. He'd want to tell me himself.'

'It's no big deal, Alix,' Todd said bracingly. 'He's lucky to have an excuse to get out of it. Everyone gets lousy drunk and usually ends up in gaol. The bride is real lucky if the groom sobers up in time for the wedding.'

She managed a smile. 'Yes, of course. That's probably why he's done it. He'll tell me tonight, I expect. Well, I'd better get back to work.'

Going back to her own office, Alix gazed at the pattern of letters on the monitor screen, but didn't attempt to form them into words. What was happening to her? Her happy, normal world was suddenly being invaded by doubts, falling apart. But through all the turmoil of emotions that beset her, there was one shining certainty to which she held fast; she loved Rhys, loved him with all her heart and soul. And Rhys was going to marry her in just a few days so what the hell was she worrying about? Damn Lynette and her lies. And what did it matter if Rhys couldn't make his stag night? It was, after all, only a glorified term for a booze-up with his friends. Hardly the end of the world.

By telling herself things like this, Alix was able to argue herself into a better mood, and was able to smile and make a thank-you speech when she was presented with the wedding gift from everyone at work. But she was far from being her usual happy self when she met up with Kathy and the girls that night. Alix had never been drunk in her life; a bit tight perhaps, but never really drunk. That night, though, she drank more than she ever had before, and because of it had a really good time, forgetting doubts, remembering only that she would soon be Rhys's wife. Most of the girls from the office were openly envious, which was intoxicating in itself, and Kathy had to firmly put Alix into a taxi at midnight and send her home to the flat.

Alix fell into bed, blissfully wondering what would happen if Rhys came home unexpectedly and found her there. But then she remembered that Rhys wouldn't be home for a couple of days at least, and fell asleep with tears on her cheeks.

The hen party had been timed to coincide with Alix's last day at work before the wedding. Which was just as well as she slept very late the next day and felt decidedly delicate when she woke. As she travelled down to Kent, sitting on the train, Alix was unable to keep Lynette's lies out of her mind, no matter how hard she tried. And they would stay with her, she realised, until she saw Rhys again. Then he would laugh away her fears, tell her not to be such a little idiot. His very presence would be enough to reassure her. And on their wedding-night, he would not only tell her, but be able to show her just how much he loved her.

As soon as she got home, too, Alix began to forget Lynette. The house was full of wedding presents that she had to open and list, there was her dress to try on for the last time to make sure she hadn't put on—or lost—any weight, a hundred and one last-minute things to be done, to be checked and double-checked. Alix dived into them like an eager cross-channel swimmer, losing herself in the preparations, and letting her mind think of nothing else.

They had the wedding rehearsal at the cathedral, with a young clergyman having to stand in for Rhys. But Rhys had rung to apologise, to swear he'd be back in plenty of time, to say that he knew she'd understand. So what else could Alix do except say yes? She didn't tell him about Lynette's lies, didn't even, by a supreme effort of will, ask him if he loved her. Just because things had been spoiled for her, Alix saw no reason why she should inflict it on Rhys as well.

The eve of the wedding arrived, and along with it came two friends from college who were to be bridesmaids, and several relations and friends of her parents, all of whom were staying over. The house was full, as was Rhys's, and Rhys's grandparents had arranged for them all to go to a local restaurant for a buffet dinner. Rhys was due to fly in that afternoon and Alix expected him to come over straight away, or at least to phone. When he didn't she guessed that he had got caught up in talking to relations, opening presents, all the things that she'd had to do a couple of days ago, so she didn't worry. She would see him tonight at the buffet party, and although they wouldn't be alone, at least they'd be together.

Opening her wardrobe to select a dress to wear, Alix looked with excitement at all the new clothes hanging there that she'd bought for the honeymoon. Rhys had kept the destination a secret, just said that they'd spend a few days in England to recover from the wedding, then go somewhere hot and exotic. Alix guessed it would be the Seychelles, a place she'd often said she would like to go to, and had bought some gorgeous clothes. Her mother would pack them for her and she would pick them up on the way to the airport after their few days in England.

Selecting one of the new outfits in the soft blue that Rhys said looked good on her because it matched her eyes, Alix dressed carefully, her heart singing with anticipation at seeing Rhys again. She and her parents got to the restaurant early to meet all the guests, but Rhys's parents were late, which was most unusual of them. When they did arrive with all the people staying at their house, there was a troubled frown on his mother's brow which she couldn't hide behind a transparent smile.

'Rhys rang from Vilnius, Alix dear. You're not to worry, but he's going to be a little late. There's some hold-up with the plane. He might have to drive to another airport, but he'll get here as soon as he can.'

Alix blinked and clenched her fists, but she managed to smile and say, 'What a shame. We'll just have to start without him.'

He didn't turn up at the restaurant that evening, and the next morning it looked as if they might have to start the wedding without him, too!

Alix woke early and immediately shot out of bed to see what the weather was like. The climate had been kind to her, it was a perfect early summer day, cloudless and still. There was dew on the grass and flowers in the beds were opening their petals to the sun. Perfect! Her next thought was of Rhys. Had he got home OK? She ran to her other window, from which she could see his bedroom, and gave a great sigh of relief; the curtains were drawn and the window partly open. Rhys always slept with his window open, so he must have arrived home at last.

Her anxieties stilled, Alix turned back into her own room. It was too early yet to get up, but she was much too full of excitement to want to go back to sleep. More than anything she longed to see Rhys, to be alone with him for just a few minutes, to feel the comfort of his arms around her, because, despite all her efforts, the shadow of doubt still lingered in her mind.

On impulse, she quickly pulled on a tracksuit and ran through the sleeping house, let herself out and ran across the garden, the dew wet on her bare feet. She went through the gate in the hedge, picked up some small stones from the border and threw them up at Rhys's window. Nothing happened. It occurred to her that if he'd got in really late he might be heavily asleep. Well, that was just too bad; she needed him so he would have to wake, and she threw up more stones that rattled satisfactorily against the panes. Now, at last, the curtain was pulled back. A head appeared and the window was pushed wide. It wasn't Rhys; it was his grandfather.

Alix looked up at him in dismay, only now realising that his grandparents must have taken over Rhys's room. 'I'm sorry,' she hissed, not wanting to wake his wife, but the old man put his finger to his lips to stop her and motioned that he would come down.

'I'm terribly sorry,' Alix said as soon as he came to the back door. 'I—I wanted to talk to Rhys.'

'Yes, of course.' He drew her into the kitchen. 'We've got his room and his mother made up a bed for him in her sewing-room.'

'He's back, then,' she said happily. 'What time did he get here?'

'Would you like a cup of tea?' old Mr Stirling asked, picking up the kettle.

'No, thank you.' She studied his face. 'He is back, isn't he?'

Slowly he shook his head. 'I've just looked; the bed hasn't been slept in.'

'Oh, no!'

'Now don't start panicking. David has gone to the airport to pick him up, so that Rhys won't have to bother with getting his own car from the car park. We can always collect that later.'

'Have you heard from him, then?'

'Yes, he rang. Said they'd fixed the plane and he should be leaving any time.'

'When was this?'

'I'm not sure exactly, but he's definitely on his way.'

Alix looked at him. The old man had spoken firmly, but she wasn't sure if he was telling her the truth or just trying not to worry her. He was a very tall man, as all the Stirlings were, still upright and good-looking, his hair thick and silver. Would Rhys look like him when he was that age? Alix wondered, and realised with a slight shock that old Mr Stirling must still be an attractive man to women even though he'd been married for nearly sixty years. A long time to fight off the competition, she thought. But then her mind went back to the present problem and she said, 'I think I'll go back home. I'm very sorry I woke you.'

'I think that would be best. Go and get a couple more hours' sleep.'

'Will you leave a message asking Rhys to phone me the moment he gets here?'

'Yes, of course. Now, off you go.'

Alix went slowly back and got into bed, but didn't attempt to go to sleep, ready to pick up the phone at the first ring. She was still waiting when her mother tapped on the door at eight-thirty and brought in a breakfast tray. 'I thought you'd like breakfast in bed today, darling. There's quite a scramble going on in the kitchen.'

'Rhys isn't home,' Alix said dully.

'No, dear, I know; Joanne slipped over to tell me. But they're expecting him at any moment,' she added cheerfully. 'So please stop worrying; there's hours yet. Now eat your breakfast—and I mean *all* of it, Alix—and then we'll all go to the hairdresser's, as we arranged.' She pressed Alix's hand. 'It will be all right, darling; Rhys would never let you down, you know. Now, I really must go and see how they're getting on downstairs. Promise me you'll eat your breakfast.'

Alix managed a smile for her harassed mother. 'Of course.'

She ate, bathed, dressed, and joined the others, and the phone still hadn't rung. It didn't ring, either, when she was having her hair done and her face made-up. When they got back to the house there was no message waiting for them, and the anxious look in her mother's face was now plain to see. Tense now, instead of excited,

Alix went up to her room. There was still time; the wedding wasn't until one and it was only eleven. She began, slowly, to get ready. The bridesmaids were in and out of the room. Her mother came in a few times, in various stages of getting ready herself. The flowers arrived. The postman with a whole pile of cards and telegrams which were to be given to the best man. Wherever he was.

Her mother came in to put on her veil. 'You really need something to put round your neck, darling. I know Rhys was going to...' She broke off, biting her lip.

'I can wear the pearl necklace you and Dad gave me for my eighteenth birthday,' Alix said tonelessly, and fished it out of the drawer. 'Can you do it up for me?'

'Yes, of course.' Her mother did so and fixed the veil. 'Oh, darling, you look lovely. I'm so proud of you.'

Her father said the same when she went downstairs to have photographs taken with her parents and the bridesmaids. But her mother kept glancing at her watch with a worried frown. 'The cars are here. What shall we do?'

'Keep to the plan, of course,' her father answered tersely. He went to say something else, but the phone rang. Snatching up the receiver, he listened, then a great look of relief came over his face. 'It's Rhys!' he said exultantly. 'He's in England.' He held the phone out towards her. 'He wants to speak to you, Alix.'

She hesitated, then her face hardened a little. 'Tell him I'm busy,' she said shortly.

Her father looked startled. 'Er—I'm afraid she can't come to the phone at the moment, Rhys. She said she'll see you in church.' He replaced the receiver and said to the room in general, 'He's at the airport, and has arranged for a helicopter to take him to Canterbury. He's going straight to the cathedral. He'll change there.'

The hired white Rolls drove at a sedate pace through the countryside to Canterbury. Alix's father took her hand, tried to talk to her, but it was a while before she responded with anything but small, brittle smiles. By the time they got to the cathedral, though, Alix had thought up a great many excuses for Rhys, and when she walked down the aisle towards him and he turned to watch her, a boyishly rueful grin on his lips, she forgave him completely. He was there, and that was all that mattered.

From that moment on the wedding was as wonderful as she'd expected it to be. In the vestry after the ceremony, Rhys kissed her, grinned and said, 'Did you think I wasn't going to make it? You should have known I'd move heaven and earth to be here. But I'm sorry I wasn't able to give you this earlier. I wanted you to wear it today.' He took a beautiful gold locket from a box and insisted on her taking off her own necklace so that he could put the locket round her neck himself. 'There. You look indescribably beautiful, urchin.'

'So do you,' she told him, seeing him so tall and debonair in his morning suit.

That made him laugh, and he kissed her again before tucking her arm in his and leading her back down the aisle as his wife.

The reception was great; Alix enjoyed every minute and hardly wanted to leave, she was having such a good time. At last she was able to show Rhys off to her college friends as she'd always wanted; and to stand beside him as they talked to friends, to dance with him as everyone looked on and clapped, was absolute heaven.

At last they left to go back to their respective houses to change and collect the luggage they would need. They said their goodbyes, with both mothers in tears and Alix close to it, and got in the car, alone at last, to drive to the country hotel that Rhys had chosen.

After dinner there, they went up to their room. Alix had wondered countless times what it would be like the first time they made love. She was a little tense and nervous, but Rhys had a bottle of champagne waiting, which helped. He undressed her himself, slowly, his eyes and hands going over her, kissing her a lot along the way. It was wonderful, exquisite, but Alix wished now that she'd never tried to seduce him, so that this would have been the first time he'd ever seen her like this.

When she was naked, he said softly, 'Aren't you going to undress me?'

She did so, but nowhere near as skilfully as he; her hands were shaking with anticipation, and he kept kissing her which made her stop what she was doing. In the end Rhys laughed and finished the task for her. She was trembling now, her eyes huge, very apprehensive but determined to be all that he wanted.

Rhys's eyes went over her, making her blush. With a small laugh, he picked her up and carried her to the bed. 'My sweet little Alix,' he murmured as he kissed her neck, her shoulder, and on down. 'So untouched. So innocent. I've dreamed of awakening you.'

His hands caressed her, setting her senses aflame, driving out all fear, until she moaned in yearning for him, arching her hot, aching body towards him. Rhys's own eyes darkened with desire and he took her then. At first it hurt so much that she cried out and tried, briefly, to fight him off, but he persisted and soon the pain was gone and it was all that she'd ever imagined, and so much, so much more. Her cry now was one of wonder, of rising excitement, peaking in a long moan of ecstasy as Rhys, too, let out a long sigh of fulfilment.

Afterwards she went to the bathroom to wash, then came back and cuddled up to him. 'Happy, urchin?' Rhys asked, kissing her.

'Oh, yes. Oh, Rhys, I never dreamed it would be so wonderful. Are you very experienced?'

He laughed at that. 'Have some more champagne. Where's your glass?'

She obediently sipped hers, but Rhys drank his down and refilled his glass. He was looking tired; but then he'd hardly slept in the last twenty-four hours in his efforts to get home. But, tired or not, he made love to her again before he fell asleep. And again, it was good, perhaps even better, for her.

Alix fell asleep in Rhys's arms, as she'd so often wished, and thought her life complete, that the human experience of love and contentment could be no greater than this. When she woke in the night, she lay still in the dark, supremely happy just to be with him and listen to him breathe, until she fell asleep again. But when she woke the second time light was creeping through the curtains and she could see that Rhys wasn't there. He had booked a suite and the door between the two rooms was closed. Getting out of bed, Alix pulled on a robe and went to look for him.

He was sitting in an armchair, talking on the phone. 'Yes, but you must pursue that,' he was saying tersely. 'Don't let up on him. We need to get the option on that——' He broke off abruptly as he saw Alix in the doorway. Then said, 'Look, I've got to go. Take this number in case of emergency.' He gave it, then put down the phone. 'Hello, urchin. I hope I didn't wake you.'

'No. I missed you. Who were you calling?'

'The team in Lithuania.'

'Do you have to let work intrude on tonight of all nights?' she demanded, feeling hurt.

'Just to let them know I've arrived safely,' he soothed. 'They were worried I wouldn't make it.' He held out his hand to her. 'Come here.'

She didn't believe him, but went to him and he pulled her down on his lap. 'My sweet little Alix,' he said softly.

'I can hardly believe we're really married.'

'Nor I.' He laughed. 'But as a married man I have some duties to carry out.'

'Oh, really? What duties?'

'Well, this for a start.' And he loosened the knot of her robe and put his hand inside, caressing her breasts, watching her lips part in desire. 'And this,' he said, as he bent to kiss them.

They made love again, and when they finally woke it was almost ten o'clock, but Rhys insisted on having breakfast brought to them in bed. The weather was beautiful again. They went for a walk to a pub, had a leisurely lunch, then went back to the room. 'I seem to remember,' Rhys said, his voice teasing, 'that you once joined me in the shower,' and he chased her into the bathroom, out of her clothes, and into the shower again. And this time it ended as it should have, with him making love to her with soap still running down their bodies.

Afterwards Rhys towelled her dry and they lay together on the bed. To lie like this with him, in broad daylight, still made Alix feel a little shy. Turning on to her stomach, she propped herself up on her elbows. Rhys had his eyes closed so she was able to look at him, marvelling at his leanness, at the strength in his shoulders and arms. But soon she wanted to touch, to explore. Leaning over him, she let her fingers run lightly over him, following the veins in his arms, the white mark low on his waist where his suntan ended and the marks on his legs where it began again. That had an effect on him which made her catch her breath.

'Sex-cat,' Rhys half-growled, his eyes still closed.

'Really?' she said, inordinately pleased, and touched him again.

Rhys grinned. 'I'm beginning to think you could soon become a tease. Come here.'

She moved closer and lay half over him, but then Rhys pulled her fully on top of him, which he hadn't done before. He wanted her and held her so that she knew it. During the last eighteen hours Rhys had made love to her only four times, but already her body was sensuously awakened to the delights of love and fulfilment. She had found what her body had instinctively craved and now would always go on needing. Putting his hands low on her hips he moved her against him, instantly lighting the fires he had brought to life and left softly burning, ready to react instantly at such a moment as this.

His face tensed, his jaw hardened, as his own libido heightened. He let go with one hand, lifted the other to cup her breast. 'My sweet Alix,' he murmured thickly. 'You have so much to learn. There's so much that I must teach you.'

'T-teach me, then,' she said on a gasping moan. 'I just want to make you happy. To make you feel the— the way you make me.'

He wound his legs round hers, holding her firmly against him, then put his hands in her hair as he brought her head down so that he could kiss her, a fierce kiss of need and passion. She returned the kiss exultantly, instinctively feeling that their lovemaking was reaching new heights, that for the first time he *had* to have her, that he wasn't just being the dutiful bridegroom. This time she had awakened his own animal need, and he wasn't to be denied.

Alix had thought it wonderful before, but it had been nothing like this. She was almost afraid of the great surges of pleasure that engulfed her and seemed to go on forever. Rhys's body thrust beneath her and his fingers tightened on her skin as his own excitement grew. Dimly she heard a ringing sound but thought it was a crazy peal of bells in her own head. Then Rhys swore and grew still and she knew it was the phone.

'Leave it! Leave it!' She managed to get the words out although it was hard to breathe. Alix moved on him again, willing him to go on and carry them both to the peak of fulfilment, but with a groan he pulled her off him and turned on his side to answer the phone.

She lay still, hardly able to believe it. Then a great rage filled her and Alix reached over him and tried to pull the phone out of Rhys's hand. He looked startled, but quickly dropped the receiver into his other hand and caught her wrist, holding her off. He was talking to someone, trying to answer a question. Furious beyond words, Alix bit his arm, digging her teeth in, making him let her go. Rhys swore again, and covered up the receiver.

'Alix, please. Can't you understand that this is an emergency? I have to——'

But she swung off the bed and into the bathroom, slamming the door behind her and bolting it. Still furious, she ran a bath and got into the water, then began to cry. So now she knew; his damn job was so important to him that Rhys would even stop making love to deal with it. And on the first day of their honeymoon, too. Fresh tears ran down her cheeks as she remembered that it had started to be so wonderful, and for Rhys, too. She saw now that, though he had of course climaxed before when he'd made love to her, there hadn't been the urgency that he had felt just now. Because of her inexperience she had thought it had been as fantastic those first few times for him as it had been for her. Now she knew that she had touched only the edge of the volcano; that the red-hot core had yet to be experienced. For Rhys, too, perhaps. But he had let a damn job intervene, so perhaps it hadn't been so wonderful for him after all.

Again the seeds of doubt that Lynette had sown in her mind, forgotten since that moment she had seen Rhys in the cathedral, all came surging back, fuelled a hundredfold. She had said nothing to him of Lynette's accusations, not wanting to spoil things, but now Rhys had spoilt it all himself.

It was almost ten minutes before he tried the bathroom door, found it locked, and banged on it. 'Alix? Alix, open the door.' She didn't answer, her mouth set into a tight line of stubbornness. 'Don't be like this, urchin,' Rhys said coaxingly. 'Come on, don't be silly.'

'I'm having a bath,' she called out coldly.

'Then let me in and I'll wash your back.'

Alix thought what would happen if she did. Washing her back was bound to lead to lovemaking, as it had done in the shower. But it wouldn't be the same; there wouldn't be the spontaneity that had started to grow into something really good between them before the damn phone rang. Remembering it, Alix said shortly, 'I can wash my own back.'

'Alix, stop being childish. Open the door,' Rhys ordered.

That angered her even more; did he think of her as a child, then? 'Go to hell!' she called out fiercely.

There was silence. Alix didn't know whether to be pleased or sorry. She lay in the bath for a long time but had to get out eventually because the skin on her fingers and toes had started to wrinkle. She dried herself, did her hair with the blow-dryer and put some make-up on. There was nothing more she could do; she would have to go out and face him.

When she did it was a complete anticlimax. Rhys had dressed and was sitting at the writing-table in the sitting-room, absorbed in reading some papers from his briefcase. Alix didn't even know he'd brought it with him! She saw him through the open door leading from the bedroom, but she went to the wardrobe to take out some clothes.

Rhys heard her and came to lean against the door jamb. 'Recovered?' he queried. Alix didn't answer. She put on her panties and was about to pull on her bra, but he came up behind her, and said, 'Let me do that for you.'

'I can manage, thanks,' she said shortly, and reached behind her to do up the clasp.

Rhys's hands were there first, and did the job neatly, as adept as when he had taken it off. A surge of resentment ran through her; at his skill that could only have come with much knowledge of women, at his high-handed assertion of his right to watch her dressing, and the way he was now putting his hands on her waist and lightly kissing her neck. Expecting that just kissing her would make her become putty in his hands again, she supposed.

'You know, urchin, you have the most beautiful body.'

She pulled away from him. 'Don't let me keep you from your work,' she said pointedly.

His eyes drawing into a frown, Rhys watched her as she pulled on a dress. 'You're behaving extremely childishly, Alix. The team need my advice. You know the project in Lithuania is at crisis point.'

'Is it? Is that why you left it till the very last minute to get back for the wedding? I wonder you were able to tear yourself away! I also wonder if there really was a problem with the plane, or whether you just invented it as an excuse for staying on yet another day.'

Rhys's mouth hardened. 'You're being ridiculous. Admittedly I wouldn't have chosen this time for the wedding if I'd been consulted. This project is important to me, and the company. But you wheedled Todd into taking me off it, so I went along with that. There was little choice. But don't expect me not to worry about it. You can't just switch off a very important part of your life, Alix.'

'No, *you* obviously can't. And it's equally obvious that I definitely take second place to your work.'

'Now, that really is ridiculous. You're my wife, Alix— of course you come first.' He smiled, reached out and caught her wrist, drew her to him and put his arms round her, still holding her wrist, imprisoning her arms behind her. 'I'm sorry, urchin,' he breathed as he kissed her throat. 'That phone rang at just the wrong moment, didn't it? I loved what we were doing. Was it good for you, too?'

His lips were sensuous against her skin, caught her earlobe, tugged at it gently. She sighed, relaxed, and closed her eyes for a moment. His grip tightened and she opened her eyes in time to see a gleam of triumph in Rhys's. It was quickly gone, as he said, 'We must try it again tonight, when we'll be sure not to be interrupted.' He began to kiss her lips in tantalising little kisses. 'Would you like that, urchin? You're such a good pupil—and there's so much I want to teach you.'

He lifted his head to look at her, waiting for her answer, confident of the reply, but she disconcerted him by saying, 'Do you love me, Rhys?'

She watched him eagerly, saw his eyebrows flicker. With a small laugh he said, 'Dearest, urchin—haven't I made you my wife?'

It might have been answer enough for him, but to Alix it was no answer at all, not when her mind had been poisoned by Lynette. She had wanted reassurance but had found only prevarication. Moving away from him, she said, 'I'm starving hungry. Where are we going to eat tonight?'

'In the hotel, I should think. I doubt if there will be many other places open on a Sunday evening.' He gave her one of his lazy smiles. 'You always did have a healthy appetite.' Taking her hand again he raised it to his lips to kiss. 'Have you forgiven me, urchin? It was disappointing for me, too, you know.'

She managed to smile in return. 'Yes, of course. When do they start serving dinner?'

Rhys laughed and hugged her. 'That's my girl.' He ran a hand over his chin. 'Now that you've at last come out of the bathroom, I'd better shave.'

He did so, put on a suit, and they went down to dinner. Rhys ordered champagne to drink with the meal.

'How extravagant,' Alix remarked.

'You only ever have one honeymoon—and it's going to be champagne all the way,' Rhys said with a grin. 'Nothing is too good for my lovely wife.'

Heady words and heady wine. Both should have gone to Alix's head, but both fell flat. But she tried to be bright and happy, because he was still Rhys and she still loved him, but there was a strangely cold feeling inside her that no amount of trying would dispel. Perhaps Rhys sensed it, because he was wonderful during that meal, attentive, devastatingly charming, setting out to amuse and captivate her, far more than he had ever done before. And he could do it, too; soon he had her laughing and wildly, hopefully, thinking that maybe she'd been making a fuss over very little. Alix also thought that defying him might have shaken Rhys a little, which seemed to be proved when, near the end of the meal, he reached across the table to take her hands in his, leaned forward and said, his eyes suggestive, 'Telling me to go to hell, indeed! My own wife! You deserve to be taken across my knee and spanked for that.'

She looked into his eyes and knew exactly what he was thinking. Alix's heart thumped with excited anticipation, and she longed to be in bed with him again, in his arms, making love. It must have showed in her face, because Rhys smiled and kissed the tips of her fingers, his eyes, so warm and evocative, holding hers.

The waiter came up and Alix drew back, her face flushing. Rhys wasn't embarrassed at all, only letting go of her hands when she pulled away, and turning a calm face to the waiter.

'Mr Stirling, there's a telephone call for you, sir.'

'Thanks. I'll take it up in my suite.' He turned to Alix whose face had tensed and waved an admonishing finger at her. 'Now don't go thinking this is work. My father promised to phone to confirm our honeymoon flight times. I'm arranging to meet him at the airport so he can take my car back home for me; it needs some work done on it while we're away.' He rose. 'Be back shortly.'

Alix sat alone for a few minutes, then it occurred to her that she wanted to ask about the photos that had been taken at the wedding. Perhaps Rhys's father could bring them to the airport with him so that she could see them. She ran upstairs to the suite, then remembered that Rhys had the key, but she had the one to the bedroom, so she went in that way, not bothering to turn on the light. The door between the two rooms was ajar and she could hear Rhys speaking.

'Look, there's only one thing for it,' he was saying. 'I'll have to come back and deal with the problems myself. Yes, I know, but it will only mean postponing our honeymoon trip for a few days until I've sorted it out, then you'll be able to handle the rest of it yourself. I can't come tonight, though; it will have to be tomorrow if I can manage it. If not, definitely the day after. Get the meetings lined up for me, will you? Whatever happens I'm determined to see this project through.'

He said goodbye, put the phone down, then turned as she opened the door and came into the room.

Her face very white and tense, Alix said, 'No! I won't let you go.'

Rhys's jaw hardened. 'I'm sorry, Alix. Please try to understand. I have to go back. It will only——'

'How can you even *contemplate* leaving me when we're on our honeymoon?' she cried, her heart breaking.

He moved towards her. 'Alix, sweetheart, I know it's a hell of a time, but it will only be for a few days and then I'll be entirely yours. I promise. I——'

He went to reach out for her but she backed away. 'No! Don't touch me!' She stared at him, feeling ice take over the warmth of her heart. 'All right. All right, then *go*. But don't expect me to be around when you get back. If you walk out on me now, then our marriage is over!'

CHAPTER SIX

RHYS laughed, not taking her seriously. But that was a mistake, because Alix had never been more serious about anything in her life. Coming up to her, he took hold of her arms and said with all his persuasive charm, 'I know you're disappointed; so am I. But I'm afraid it just can't be helped, urchin. I'll take you home tomorrow and be back before you know it.'

'You're right, I won't know it—because I won't be there,' she said, her mouth set into a cold, unhappy line.

He frowned. 'I'm not doing this on purpose, Alix. If you hadn't persuaded Todd to take me off this project I——'

'I didn't,' she interrupted. 'It was his idea. He said he'd go to Lithuania himself if necessary.' Her lip curled. 'He actually thought you *wanted* to get married, that you *wanted* time for a honeymoon. It seems he and I were both wrong!'

'Of course I wanted to get married,' Rhys said roughly.

'Really? Or was it because it was a condition of you taking over Todd's job?'

The question came out so unexpectedly, so bluntly, that Rhys wasn't able to hide the fleeting flash of consternation that came into his eyes. He covered it, but not quite quickly enough. Alix felt something die inside her: her innocence, her belief in love.

'Rubbish! What on earth gave you that idea?' Rhys demanded, his voice forceful.

126

She didn't answer, just pulled free and walked into the bedroom. The suitcases were stacked on a rack in the corner. Alix pulled Rhys's off and threw it on to the bed. 'What are you waiting for?' she said curtly. 'If you hurry you can get there in the company plane tonight. Here, I'll help you.' And going to the wardrobe she began to pull his clothes out and throw them on the suitcase.

Rhys strode round to her and gripped her wrists. 'Alix, stop this! All right, I know how devastated you are. But I swear I'll make it up to you. And I don't have to go now. We can have tonight together. Go to bed now, this minute. We can make love all night.' He gave a soft laugh and tried to kiss her neck. 'You'll be so sated with love that you'll be glad to get rid of me.'

In a great surge of cold fury, Alix pushed him away. 'Go to bed with *you*?' she said contemptuously. 'I'd rather *die*!'

He stared at her, brought up short by the disgust in her face. 'Urchin, I——'

But she had walked over to the phone, picked it up, and said to the receptionist, 'Would you please call a taxi to take Mr Stirling to the airport? And have his bill made up, please; he'll be checking out immediately. Yes, I'll be leaving, too. Thank you.'

As soon as she put the phone down, Rhys, his mouth tight, said, 'Alix, please try to calm down. I know you're upset but——'

'On the contrary,' she said shortly. 'I'm perfectly calm. Well, what are you waiting for? Why don't you pack? Are you thinking that that's part of a wife's duties? Pity—because you haven't got one any more!'

'Alix, this is crazy.' Catching hold of her arms as she went to stride past him, Rhys looked down at her, his eyes angry and his mouth drawn into a hard line. 'All right, you've made your point. I thought that working for the company would make you understand how important the project is to me, but you obviously don't—and you're damn well not going to try to understand. So, OK. You win. You're right and our honeymoon should take precedence over everything else. I've got my priorities wrong. So I'll phone Todd and get him to go out to Vilnius in my place. We'll go on with our honeymoon as we planned.'

He looked at her expectantly. Expecting what? she wondered. For her to smile and throw herself in his arms, completely happy again. For everything to be as it was before, except that he would be bearing a grudge, playing the martyr, for the rest of their honeymoon, for the rest of their lives! Picking up her own case, Alix began to toss things into it, the beautiful new clothes, all thrown in haphazardly. 'You can do what you like,' she said curtly. 'I'm leaving.'

'No, you're not. I won't let you.'

Alix laughed stridently. 'It's too late for the possessive husband bit. You just proved that you couldn't care less.'

'That isn't true, Alix.' Rhys tried to catch hold of her again, but she turned round with such blazing anger in her eyes that he drew back, his own eyes startled. But he said forcefully, 'I mean it, Alix. I do care about you; you know that.'

'Care?' She paused, a dress on a hanger in her hands as she considered the word. 'Yes, I believe you do care for me.'

'Well, then?'

But she went on, 'I think you care for me because I've always been around, and you married me because you thought you could mould me into the obedient sort of wife you wanted: someone who wouldn't mind you going off during the honeymoon, for example. And if I thought you really loved me, then maybe I wouldn't mind. Maybe I'd understand. But you don't love me. You don't even know what love means. And I'm not going to stick around just to be used by you, to be kept sweet by sex, the way I've been kept sweet by kisses for the last eighteen months. I've grown up, Rhys. I see through you. So go to Vilnius. Go any place you damn well want. You've got what you wanted—a wife so you can take over Todd's job. You've got a marriage licence and a stack of wedding photos to prove it.' She drew herself up, chin high. 'But that's all you've got. Because I won't be around any more.'

Rhys was gazing at her, a strange, punch-drunk sort of look in his eyes. 'Alix?' He said her name on a hoarse, questioning note, almost as if he couldn't believe it was her.

The phone rang.

'That will be your taxi. You don't want to keep it waiting.' Alix flung the last of her things into her case and shut it. Picking up her bag and the car keys, she said, 'I'll give the keys back to your father. Goodbye, Rhys. I hope your project goes well for you.'

She turned towards the door, but he seemed to come back to life and caught hold of her. 'No, I'm not going to let you go like this. Alix, we have to talk. We have to——'

'The only thing I want to talk to you about is a divorce!' And she strode out of the door while Rhys was still standing staring at her with stunned disbelief in his face.

* * *

The car enclosed her. It was warm and comforting like a cocoon. Alix could well understand how people who committed suicide chose to do so in their cars; it was almost like going full circle, from one womb to another. She had been driving a long time and her eyes were aching with tiredness. She had absolutely no idea where she was, had just kept driving. Soon, she realised, she would be too tired to go on and would have to find somewhere to stop, but almost immediately fate made the decision for her because the car engine sputtered and gradually died as it ran out of petrol. Alix steered it on to the grass verge at the side of the road and turned off the ignition. It was a quiet, unlit road, with trees on either side. Alix got into the back seat, locked the doors, and curled up as best she could, then gave way at last to tears, crying for all those years of dreams that had so soon turned into a nightmare.

Daylight finally woke her from a restless, troubled sleep. Her dress, the one she'd put on to have dinner with Rhys last night, was terribly crumpled and looked completely out of place. Getting her suitcase out of the boot, Alix found trousers, a shirt and a sweater, a pair of trainers to take the place of her high heels, and went behind a bush to change into them. She went to brush her hair but found that she'd left all her make-up stuff behind in the bathroom at the hotel. Well, at least she'd remembered to bring her handbag; she'd be able to buy some more. But first she'd have to get some petrol for the car. Cleaning up her face as best she could, she began to walk down the road.

The nearest village was over three miles away. Alix walked down the hill towards its centre and paused, enraptured by the scene despite all her problems. There was a village green with a pond that was the home to a great many ducks, a pair of ancient stocks black with age, an old church, pretty stone houses, two or three bow-fronted shops, one of which advertised cream teas and morning coffee. The thought of coffee created an immediate longing for it. But it was early yet, the village only just awakening.

Across the other side of the village green a milk float appeared, jangling along. Alix walked over to it and waited till the milkman came up with his hands full of empties. 'Excuse me.'

'Morning, miss.'

'Is there a garage in the village, please. Somewhere I can get some petrol?'

'Yes, just down the side road there.' The milkman glanced at his watch. 'But you're too early yet; it doesn't open till eight. Run out of petrol, have you?'

Alix nodded. 'I'll sit on the seat over there and wait. Thanks for your help.'

The milkman went on with his round, came to the tea-shop where a woman opened the door to him. He stood talking to her for a few minutes, then turned and called out to Alix, beckoning her over.

'We thought you might like a cup of tea while you're waiting,' the woman said with a smile.

Alix accepted gratefully, in such an emotional state that she was almost moved to tears by their kindness. She sat in the café by the window, only half listening as the woman chatted to her while she got the place ready for the day, telling her what a busy weekend they'd had. 'And us short-handed, too. One of my girls has sprained her wrist; it'll be another three weeks before she can come back to work. And I can't find anyone to take her place—

young girls don't want to work in a little village like this, they all want to be off to offices in the town. But you can't blame them, really,' she added large-mindedly. 'They have all the shops to go round in the town. We get lots of sightseers here, because it's so pretty, but there's nothing for the youngsters.'

The woman insisted on giving her a sandwich to eat, but Alix had to force it down, her appetite gone. When she'd finished she went into the ladies room to wash her face and comb her hair with her fingers, then insisted, in turn, on paying for the food. The garage was open and the proprietor let her have a can of petrol, but apologetically said he couldn't run her back to her car as he was expecting a couple of customers to arrive shortly and he had no one with him.

Feeling a little better after the food, Alix began the long walk back to the car, and it was only now that she began to think about the future. But it was all too raw and painful for her to make any important decisions; all she knew was that she wanted to hide away somewhere for a while to lick her wounds, to give herself time to recover a little so that she could think clearly. Reaching the car, Alix put in the petrol, then drove back to the village to return the can. Again she was struck by what a peaceful place it looked, then remembered that the woman at the tea-rooms needed an assistant for three weeks, almost exactly the time Alix had off work for her honeymoon.

Recognising an act of fate when it rose up and hit her, Alix went back to Jemima's Tea-Rooms and offered her services, which were soon accepted. Within an hour Alix was helping in the kitchen, her case safely stowed away in a small bedroom upstairs, the thoughts of her two-day marriage necessarily pushed to the back of her mind as she started a completely new way of life.

Despite all her problems, Alix found that she actually enjoyed those three weeks. She was kept busy all day long, serving morning coffees, cooking lunches, serving teas in the afternoons, and in the evening baking the home-made cakes for the next day. The cordon bleu cookery course that she'd taken so that she could make delicious meals for Rhys gave her the confidence to take over the cooking and she added several dishes to the lunchtime menu, which drew in more customers. At night, instead of lying in bed thinking about Rhys, Alix fell into an exhausted sleep and was able to face the day ahead.

After a couple of days it occurred to her that it was the day she and Rhys should have called at their respective homes to collect their luggage for the trip abroad. She didn't know whether Rhys had told their parents what had happened, but she didn't want them to be worried about her, so that evening she rang her home from a call-box in the village.

Her mother's voice, sharp with relief, immediately warned her that Rhys had told them. 'Alix, where are you? We've been so worried.'

'I'm quite all right. Really.'

'Why didn't you come home, darling? It was so wrong of Rhys to go away like that.'

'He went to Vilnius, then?'

'Yes, darling, I'm afraid he did. But he was most concerned about you when he rang to tell us. He expected you to be here and wanted to talk to you. Where are you? Are you with a friend?'

'Yes.'

'What's the telephone number?'

'The number's out of order,' Alix lied. 'I'm calling from a phone-box.'

'Come home, darling. Promise me you'll be here tomorrow. Alix, please promise,' she repeated when Alix didn't answer.

'No, I'm sorry, I don't want to come home yet. I need time to think.'

Her voice full of anger, her mother said, 'I could kill Rhys for doing this to you. How insensitive to leave you like that.'

'Well, now I've left him,' Alix said shortly. 'For good.'

'What?' There was a stunned note in her mother's voice. 'Oh, Alix, no! Please don't be hasty. I know that Rhys has upset you, anyone would be upset, but you mustn't let it spoil your life. Look, Rhys is due home again shortly; let him come and see you so that you can talk it through. I know he's very sorry for what happened and——'

Alix's laugh, full of irony, cut her short. 'I have no wish to talk to Rhys or to see him. As far as I'm concerned our marriage—if you can call it that—is over. Goodbye, Mother. Give my love to Daddy.'

'No, wait! Alix, your father is here, he wants to talk to you.'

'I'm sorry.' Alix was suddenly crying. 'I—I can't...' Quickly she put the phone down, unable to control herself any longer, then leant against the glass doors, dissolved in tears.

Mrs Pegram, the owner of the tea-rooms, saw her tear-stained face when she came in, but wasn't the sort to ask questions. Alix went up to her room and took the wedding- and engagement-rings from the drawer where she'd put them soon after she'd arrived. She looked at them for a long time, then went down to the tiny office, found a box and some cotton-wool, and made up a parcel of the rings, addressed to Rhys's flat in London. The next morning she got the milkman to take it to the nearest town to post for her.

At first, during those weeks, Alix's thoughts were chaotic, veering from one idea about what to do, then to another. The thought of staying on at the tea-rooms forever was sometimes extremely attractive, but Mrs Pegram only wanted her for three weeks. OK, so she could open her own café or restaurant somewhere else. But the difficulties of that soon pushed it out of her mind. She thought of going abroad to live, of starting a new life under a new name, cutting herself off from ever having to see Rhys again. But Alix loved her parents very much and knew she could never bear to be so far away from them. And, anyway, why the hell should she cut herself off? It was Rhys who had behaved like a prize chauvinist pig, not her. Why should she disrupt her life because of him? she thought in deep indignation.

OK, so she'd stay in England, Alix decided. But she still didn't want to see Rhys, which would mean giving up her job. It was another week before she acknowledged that it was a good job which she enjoyed, so why should she give it up and make herself unemployed, for heaven's sake? Better, surely, to stay there until she could find another position. Rhys was seldom there, anyway. And if she had to face him, so what? Presumably she'd have to face him some time; their parents still lived next door to one another. It had to be done so she might just as well get it over with.

The three weeks over, Alix said goodbye to Mrs
Pegram, got in the car and headed for London, her self-
esteem extremely battered but not lost. There were still
several days before she was due back at work. Alix went
to a staff agency and let them know she was looking for
a new job, then went to a different agency who found
her a furnished flat at a reasonable rent which she could
move into at once. Clothes were the next problem. Alix
toyed with the cowardly idea of just buying new ones,
but she'd spent a great deal on her honeymoon outfits
and didn't have much left in her bank account after
paying three months in advance for the flat. So she drove
down to Kent on a day when she knew both fathers would
be at work and both mothers out doing voluntary work
by delivering meals on wheels to old people in the neigh-
bouring town. Her only fear was that Rhys might be
around, but, as she realised cynically, he had probably
gone back to Lithuania by now, if he had really come
back at all.

After a difficult journey in which she seemed to get
caught in an endless traffic jam on the motorway, Alix
let herself into the house and ran up to her room. Time
was getting short; she would have to hurry. Her suitcases, bought specially for the honeymoon, were standing
packed and ready. Ignoring them, Alix took out her old
cases and began to pack them with her working clothes.
She noticed a large envelope on the table beside her bed,
one she certainly hadn't left there herself. She finished
packing the cases, pulled out a hold-all and put her shoes
in, but then curiosity got the better of her and she picked
up the envelope, emptying the contents on the bed. It
contained the proof copies of the wedding photos.

Dozens of them dropped out on to the quilt: her alone, with her parents, the bridesmaids—with Rhys.

Standing staring down at them, Alix didn't notice a car that drove by, pulled up with a jerk and then backed up, blocking the driveway. Rhys got out, ran up to the car she'd been using and put his hand on the bonnet, felt that it was still warm. He glanced at the house, ran to the front door but found it locked, so went round to the back. The sound of breaking glass broke through Alix's absorption. Her first thought was that it must be a burglar and she grabbed the telephone, but then heard Rhys's voice. 'Alix? Alix, where are you?'

Her heart filled with horror. No! She couldn't see him. She wouldn't. She made a move to lock herself in, but stopped short. What good would that do? He wouldn't go away and it would all become ridiculous, with her on one side of the door and him on the other. A new thought filled her with dread; if he'd broken a window to get in the house, then he might even break down her door. She looked wildly round, saw the photographs on the bed, then quickly went out on to the landing, closing the door behind her so that he couldn't see inside.

Rhys came running up the stairs, turned and saw her as he reached the top. Without hesitation, he strode to her and took her in his arms, held her close. 'Thank God you've come home! I've been so worried about you, urchin. Don't ever do that to me again. I've...' He became aware of her stiffness within his arms and broke off, stepped back to look at her.

'Let go of me,' she ordered curtly.

A look of chagrin came into his eyes, but Rhys kept his hands on her arms as he said, 'So I'm to be punished even more, am I? Well, I admit I deserve it, but if you only knew what I—what we all—have been going through these last weeks. Oh, Alix, sweetheart, I've been going mad with worry.'

'Really? Made a couple of phone calls from Vilnius when you weren't busy, did you?'

His mouth twisted at the sarcasm in her tone, but Rhys said, 'I was only there for a few days; I got back as soon as I could. I mean it, Alix. I've missed you like crazy. You really made me——'

But she moved away from him. 'I'm really not interested,' she said coldly. 'You can leave by the front door.'

'Leave?' She had gone to walk away but Rhys caught her shoulder and spun her round. 'I'm not going anywhere without you.'

She shrugged, a cold anger at his presumption that he only had to apologise and it would be all right, making her implacable. 'Suit yourself. I'll leave, then.'

'No.' He moved between her and the door of her room, looked into her face and saw the bitterness there, the flash of near hatred in her eyes. 'Alix!' He said her name on a small gasp and frowned, recognising the depth of her feelings. 'Look, we have to talk. We can't just ignore what's happened. Please.' He made a supplicatory gesture with his hand.

Reluctantly, Alix said, 'All right. What do you want to say?'

'First of all, of course, that I'm deeply sorry that you're so upset. It was entirely my fault. I was wrong; I should have let Todd take on the project from the start. But must we let this come between us? Can't we start again, Alix?' He reached out to touch her but she flinched away. A grim look came into his eyes, and Rhys added, 'After all, we are married, and nothing can change that.'

'A divorce can,' she retorted at once.

He winced. 'Isn't that being rather hasty? Isn't what we feel for each other worth more than——?' He stopped as Alix laughed.

'I don't know what *you* feel—just annoyed, I expect, because your plans have gone wrong, because I didn't turn out to be the tame puppet whose strings you could pull whenever you felt like it and then put back in the cupboard while you got on with your own life.' Her eyes blazed at him, the cold blue of an angry sea. 'But I do know what I feel for you—and that's nothing! Not love, not infatuation, not even hero-worship any more. All I do feel is anger that I was such a fool as to be taken in by you for so long.' She laughed jeeringly again. 'No wonder you didn't want me to move in with you before we were married. Why, it only took me two days to have my eyes opened, to find out what you were really like.'

Rhys's mouth hardened. 'Oh? And just what did you find out?'

'That you're completely selfish. That you married me just because you needed the accessory of a wife, and you thought I was so besotted by you that I'd do whatever you wanted, be whatever you wanted me to be.' She gave him a derisive look. 'But if you wanted that you should have married me years ago. You left it too late, Rhys. I've learnt enough to see you for what you are—and I don't like what I see.'

His jawline had hardened as she spoke, and now there was anger in Rhys's eyes as he reached out and took hold of her arms. 'No? But just what did you marry me for, Alix? Tell me that. Was it just to have your childhood

dream come true? To have a happy-ever-after ending?'
Suddenly his hands tightened and he jerked her towards
him. 'Or was it for this?' His mouth came down, hard
and insistent, taking her lips with an irresistible force,
bending her head back so that she had to open her
mouth, had to let him ravage the softness within.

Alix put her hands against his chest and tried to push
him away, but he was holding her too tightly. She made
sounds of rage deep in her throat, tried to twist her head
free but couldn't. Her efforts to escape only served to
increase his anger. He let go of her wrists but kept her
arms pinioned between them as he held her against him,
his other hand grabbing a handful of her hair so that
she could no longer even move her head. His kiss
deepened, became insistent, and masculinely demanding. Despite her fury, Alix felt the old fire take
hold, desire surge through her body, and now had to
fight that as well as Rhys. Her senses began to go; she
felt the now familiar sensation of drowning in a tide of
sensuality. Desperately she redoubled her efforts to break
free, struggling, kicking out at him. Rhys swore under
his breath, but bent her under him, so that she had to
cling to him or fall. Her body was pressed against his
now, and she was gasping, panting, her fingers digging
into his shoulders. Her fury gave way to a moan of
awakened need as she felt her last resistance crumble
before the onslaught of his lips. Rhys gave a triumphant
laugh against her mouth, stooped to pick her up, take
her to her room, her bed.

But fate decreed otherwise. The front door was flung
open with a crash as both their mothers erupted into the
hall.

'Alix!'

'Rhys!'

Rhys swore furiously and had to let Alix go.

The women saw them and came running up the stairs in time to see Alix stagger back, an appalled expression in her eyes as she realised just how near she'd come to succumbing to him. Wiping her mouth with the back of her hand, she cried out, her voice filled with venom, 'I hate you! *I hate you!*'

'Rhys, what on earth . . . ?'

Rhys swung round on the two older women. 'Damn you, did you have to interrupt us just at this moment? Didn't you have enough sense to keep out of the way?'

He turned towards Alix, made a move to go to her, but she screamed out, 'No! Don't touch me!' and ran into her room, locking the door behind her.

There were raised voices out on the landing, people knocking on the door and calling her name, but Alix took no notice. Her breath gasping and unsteady, she grabbed the phone by her bed and managed to call a taxi, telling it to wait round the corner. As quietly as possible, she opened her window, dropped her cases out, then climbed through it and down the drainpipe, a means of escape she'd used often before as a child, but not for some years. She fell the last few feet, bruising her hands, but quickly gathered up her cases and bag and pushed past the cars blocking the drive, out into the street. She hurried to the corner and round it, praying that it would be some time before they realised she wasn't just sulking and had gone.

It was a close thing; the taxi came and she threw her cases and herself into it, telling the driver to go, go! As it turned the far corner she risked a glance back and saw Rhys run into the street, looking for her. She had intended to take the taxi just to the station to catch the next train to London, but guessed that Rhys would immediately go there, so instead she asked the driver to take her all the way to London. He agreed willingly enough, but she had an uncomfortable journey, continually looking out of the back window in case Rhys's car appeared, only relaxing when they reached the outskirts of London and the streets got busy.

Alix hid in her flat for the next three days like a fox driven into its lair and with the hounds baying outside, too frightened to come out. But Monday morning came and she was due to go back to work. By then she had managed to work herself up into a state of cold anger against Rhys again. But there was a desperate undertone to it, because now she knew that she was still vulnerable to him, that he had the power to overcome her anger and arouse her sexually, that she didn't have the strength to resist him. So she would just have to make sure that he didn't get near to her again, that she kept him at a distance with words and open hatred.

When she walked into the office it was obvious that no one there had any idea what had happened. Todd and Brenda greeted her with big grins and wanted to know why they hadn't received a postcard.

'The post must be slow,' Alix prevaricated.

'Or you were too busy,' Todd said with a knowing grin. 'Will you be free to go to Alaska with me in a couple of weeks?'

'Yes, of course.'

Todd raised an eyebrow. 'Don't you want to check with Rhys first?'

'No.' She tried not to let anything show in her face.

'Come to an understanding about work, have you?'

'You could say that.'

He nodded and half turned away, then stopped and said, 'That reminds me; I must remember to book you on the passenger list as Mrs Stirling now that you've changed your name. I take it you've had your passport changed?'

Alix shook her head and said quickly, 'No, I haven't. And I'd much rather you went on using my maiden name. It—it's a matter of principle,' she added lamely.

'I suppose you mean it's the latest fashion to keep your own name,' Todd observed. 'OK, if that's what you want.' He grinned. 'Or until Rhys persuades you to change your mind.'

Alix managed to smile back but was glad when he went into his own room. Brenda took the day's post in to him and Alix went into her own office to hang up her jacket. She looked round the room, thinking how happy she'd been the last time she'd been there. But no, not entirely happy, because by then Lynette had already told her the truth about Rhys, a truth she had been too stupid to even contemplate let alone accept. Trying to push these unhappy thoughts out of her mind, Alix sat down at her desk to catch up with the reports that Brenda had left on it, but the phone rang almost at once. It was Kathy.

'Hi, I heard you were back. Well? Did you have a wonderful time? Is Rhys everything he's rumoured to be?'

Faced with such direct questions, Alix didn't know how to answer. Back at the flat, as she mentally prepared herself for today, she had struggled with the problem of how much to tell people. It was going to be so difficult, working in the same place as Rhys. The coldness between them was sure to be noticed. Except that Rhys was bound to go away again almost immediately. So Alix had decided to pretend that nothing had happened, but here was Kathy, who was one of her closest friends, and now she would have to lie to her. Alix badly needed a shoulder to cry on, but had the sense to recognise that Kathy was the last person to confide in, so instead she managed to say brightly, 'Oh, hi, Kathy. Yes, I had a wonderful time, but don't expect me to tell you anything else; that's personal. Anyway, how are you? Fill me in on all the gossip that's being going around while I've been away.' And so she managed to fob Kathy off, and several other girls who rang or dropped into her office, agog with curiosity.

Alix wondered grimly what they were so curious about; did they expect her to look different? Or did they really expect her to tell them what a fantastic lover Rhys was? That he lived up to his reputation? Thinking about the few times they had made love, she supposed that he was a great lover, not that she had anything to compare him with. But he had certainly lifted her to the heights of excitement, time and time again. Was that what made a man a good lover—being able to please the woman he was with? And had he been pleased with her? Hardly, she had been far too inexperienced. There had just been that once when he seemed really aroused and . . .

Hastily Alix dragged her thoughts back to the present and bent her head over her work again.

It was mid-morning before Rhys walked into the office. He hadn't expected her to be there and was walking towards Todd's room, his mouth set into a grim line, when he glanced through the glass partition into her office and did a double-take. He sent the door flying back, startling her, and for a long moment they stared at each other, finding nothing to say.

Todd broke the silence, coming up behind Rhys and putting a hand on his shoulder. 'You're a lucky man, Rhys. Not many wives would leave their husband asleep while they go off to work.'

'Yes, aren't I?' Rhys replied with a crooked grin. 'Alix is becoming quite adept at slipping off and leaving me.'

His irony was lost on Todd, who laughed and said, 'And what's this about her still using her maiden name? I'd have thought you would have put your foot down there.'

Rhys's lips thinned. He was still standing in the doorway looking at her. Giving it a meaning that only she could understand, he said, 'Unfortunately Alix doesn't find my name to her liking. But I'm quite sure that she'll very soon come to realise that being Mrs Stirling is far more—rewarding than being Miss North. Won't you, Alix?' he added compellingly.

Her chin came up. 'I find it inconvenient,' she said coolly.

'But not for long,' Rhys stated firmly, his tone a threat, his eyes challenging.

But she said, 'Forever,' and knew, as Todd drew Rhys away, that she had taken up his challenge and issued her own.

CHAPTER SEVEN

Sitting at her desk after they'd gone, Alix felt as if she and Rhys had just declared war. Maybe they had. Her head began to ache, probably because she hadn't slept much during the last three days, but she forced herself to think. The first thing, she decided, was to make absolutely sure of her ground, so she put a call through to the parent company in Canada and spoke to the woman who acted as Todd's father's personal assistant. Alix knew the woman from her frequent trips there with Todd, so after exchanging friendly greetings and saying, yes, she'd had a wonderful honeymoon, Alix said, 'We have a man here who is interested in one of the posts you're advertising in the company newsletter. The problem is that he isn't married and he understands that, although it doesn't say so in the advert, it's company policy for all executive positions to be filled only by married men. Is that right?'

The woman gave a small groan. 'I'm afraid so, Alix. It's a big problem for us. But you know what old Mr Weston is like; he's forever going on about family men being more settled and unlikely to get into trouble when they're abroad. The firm's reputation is everything to him—he's even been known to fire people who've just got drunk!'

'Really?' Alix managed to laugh and say, 'It's a good job Rhys and I got married, then.'

146

'Well, I know Mr Weston was concerned about Rhys getting so far ahead in the company when he was still single, but as soon as Rhys got engaged to you everything was OK.'

'Wouldn't Mr Weston rather we'd got married straight away?' Alix ventured.

'Well, as Rhys pointed out, you were only twenty; he wanted to wait until you were a little older, and Mr Weston was happy to go along with that. He likes you both very much, you know.'

As they had received a very generous wedding present from him, Alix didn't doubt it. She rang off, momentarily wondering what had happened to all the presents, but the thought went out of her mind as she pondered what she'd found out. So, as she'd already accepted in her mind, Lynette had been right all along. Todd, then, had lied to her when she'd asked him. Out of kindness, she supposed, knowing how in love with Rhys she was— had once been. The two men had protected her from the truth as they would an indulged child. That idea filled her with resentment for a moment, but she had changed so much in the last few weeks that now Alix could look back on her old self with a kind of wonder at her own naivety and trustfulness. Would she have gone on through life like that, she wondered, if none of this had happened? Would she have gone on seeing everything through rose-coloured glasses and finding life perfection, the realisation of her dream? A great feeling of envy for the girl that she'd been suddenly filled her, and Alix put her head in her hands, feeling so low that she could have cried.

The sound of Todd's door opening as Rhys came out made her sit up quickly and pretend to be absorbed in her work; no way would she let Rhys see how low she was. He hesitated at her door but she kept her head down and, to her deep relief, he moved on. Ten minutes later the phone on her desk buzzed. It was her mother. Alix might have known that Rhys would immediately ring her. It wasn't a pleasant phone call. Her mother was very upset, in tears, wanting her to come home.

'No, Mum, I'm sorry. I've found a flat and I'll be living on my own from now on,' Alix said firmly.

Her mother wouldn't ring off until Alix had given her the address and telephone number. Which meant that her flat, which was to have been a haven of peace, would now become under siege, Alix thought wryly as she managed to break off the call at last.

At twelve-thirty Todd came out of his office and opened her door. 'I'm having lunch with Rhys; you want to come along?'

'No, thanks. I have some shopping to do.'

His eyes rose to heaven. 'The main occupation of the married woman—shopping; I hate it.'

'This is a different kind of shopping—for food.'

Todd grinned wickedly. 'Keeping his strength up, huh?'

She made a face at him and he laughed and went away. Alix watched him go and wondered what his reaction would be when he found out she and Rhys weren't even living together, that she was getting a divorce. Dully, she supposed that she ought to see a solicitor about that, get a legal separation or something. But at the moment she was so tired, without the strength to take on a new set of problems.

The phone rang again and Kathy said, 'Are you going to lunch with Rhys?'

'No, I——'

'See you downstairs in five minutes.'

With a sigh, Alix put on her jacket.

'Lord, how exhausted you look!' Kathy exclaimed when Alix joined her, but then stopped herself and laughed. 'Well, I suppose you would look tired. I always knew Rhys would be a stud,' she added with satisfaction.

'Kathy!' Alix pretended to be outraged, but then laughed, which was good. Alix hadn't laughed for nearly a month.

They grabbed a sandwich and then went to a nearby food store, Alix explaining away the fact that she was only buying for one by saying that Rhys was going out to dinner with a customer.

'Isn't he taking you with him to act as hostess?'

'No, men only.'

'Well, take the opportunity to have an early night. And when he comes home pretend to be asleep,' Kathy advised.

'Is that what you do?' Alix asked, momentarily curious.

'Sometimes,' Kathy admitted. 'It's hard being a career-girl and a housewife as well. There's so much to do when you get home from work and at the weekends. There are times when you need a break.'

Alix couldn't imagine pretending to the man you loved, but said, 'You never told me that before.'

'You weren't married before. You were a sweet, innocent virgin,' Kathy said flippantly.

'Did it show?'

Kathy smiled. 'It shone out of you—almost as brightly as the way you lit up whenever Rhys came into the room.'

'I didn't realise I was that transparent,' Alix said ruefully.

Studying her face for a long moment, Kathy said, 'I expected you to be really radiant now that you're married, the way you were on your wedding-day. But you're not, you're——' she struggled to find a word but then shrugged her shoulders '—I don't know, you're just not as I expected you to be.'

Alix managed a small smile. 'As you said, I'm just a bit tired, that's all.'

'And you're thinner.'

'Good; I'm on a diet,' Alix lied.

She took her purse from her bag to pay, and Kathy said, 'Hey, where are your rings? Don't tell me you've lost them already?'

'No, of course not.' Alix managed another smile. 'They've—er—gone to be altered. They didn't fit over one another.' Quickly she paid and glanced at her watch. 'We'd better be getting back.'

Rhys was in the building all afternoon, in his own department, working on the Lithuanian project, Alix supposed. She fully expected him to come to find her at the end of the day, and was surprised when he didn't, but she found out why when she got to her flat. Her father was waiting for her at the door.

He now worked in the city, too, and was still handsome in his dark business suit. 'Hello, my darling girl,' he greeted her, and gave her a hug and a kiss, almost as if she were still a small child.

Alix unlocked the door which led straight into the small sitting-room. John North looked round. 'Are you living here alone?' Alix looked at him and he said quickly, 'I mean, you're not sharing with a girlfriend?'

'No.' She shook her head. 'Would you like a coffee?'

'Have you got anything stronger?'

'Sorry, no.'

'Then a coffee will do fine.'

She went into the tiny kitchen to prepare it. Her father followed her to have a look, then went away to inspect the bedroom and small bathroom.

'It isn't much of a place, Alix,' he remarked when she rejoined him in the sitting-room.

'It's all I need and all I can afford.'

'If you're short of money, darling, you know you can always——'

'I'm not,' she interrupted, putting the cups down on a coffee-table. She sank into a chair. 'All right, Dad, get it over.'

He stood looking down at her for a moment, then pulled up a chair close to hers, sat down and took her hand. 'I think you'd better tell me what happened.'

'Didn't Rhys tell you?'

'Only that an emergency had cropped up and he'd had to go away during your honeymoon. That you were upset because of it and he couldn't contact you. He thought you were punishing him, teaching him a lesson. Which he seemed to need, I might add,' her father said drily. 'But looking at you now, I can see there's more to it than that. Won't you tell me, darling?'

Tears pricked her eyes, but Alix bit her lip and said, 'Did Mum send you to persuade me to go back to him?'

John North grinned ruefully. 'They all did. And until I saw you, that was what I intended. But not now.' His grip on her hand tightened. 'I'm on your side, Alix. Always remember that. Whatever you want to do I'll help you.'

'I want to divorce Rhys,' she said baldly.

He stared at her. 'My dear child! What did he do to you?' His face became grim and he clenched his fist. 'If he's hurt you in any way...'

'No. No, it's nothing like that,' she assured him. Alix bit her lip. 'I don't want to tell you, because you're such close friends with Uncle David and Aunt Joanne. I don't want to sp-spoil that.'

'Alix, darling, you are our daughter, our only child, and your mother and I love you more than anything in the world. Friendships mean *nothing* compared with that. You, and your happiness, is all that matters to us.'

His words were so comforting, so reassuring when she felt so alone, that Alix couldn't control the tears any longer. 'Oh, Daddy,' she sobbed, 'I found out Rhys doesn't love me. He never has. He only married me so he could get a job!'

Gathering her into his arms, her father said, 'There, there, my darling. Tell me all about it.'

She did so, brokenly, crying out her distress, then had her face wiped and was made to drink her coffee. He made her feel as if she was a little girl crying over a lost doll, which Alix, at that moment, didn't mind in the least. But when her father stood up and said angrily, 'I'm going to have this out with Rhys! How dare he treat you like this?' she immediately became a twenty-two-year-old woman again.

'No! You're not to. It's my problem, not yours. You gave me what you thought I wanted—what I *did* want at the time. It's my fault; I went ahead and married Rhys even though I'd been warned that he didn't love me. So it's up to me to sort it out.' He went to speak but she held up her hand. 'I promise that if I need you I'll be in touch. But I have to do this on my own.' She smiled rather bitterly. 'It will do me good to get myself out of a mess for once instead of having you do it for me.'

'This isn't just a scrape with the car or something, Alix.'

'I know that. It's more like a head-on crash.' She looked at him earnestly. 'But it's something I have to settle for myself. And I want you to promise that you won't say anything to Rhys's parents. It's up to him to tell them as much as he wants them to know. And promise that you won't let this break up your friendship. After all, you all acted in good faith; you thought that this was what Rhys and I both wanted. And it was; I wanted it so much.' Her voice broke. 'Please don't make it worse than it is by letting it spoil your lives, too. Promise me, Daddy.'

Her father shook his head unhappily. 'I understand what you're saying, darling. But I *have* to tell them something.'

Alix gripped the arms of her chair. 'Tell them that I was so upset that Rhys went away during out honeymoon that I just can't live with him any more.'

'It's hardly enough reason for you to break with him completely, Alix. I doubt if they'll believe it.'

She gave a tired sigh. 'Then let them think that I'm just punishing Rhys, as he said. When enough time has gone by it will be easier for them to accept the truth.'

He looked unhappy about it but nodded. 'All right, if that's what you want. Now, go and wash your face and let's go and have a meal; I'm starving.'

'No, you should go home. Mum will be waiting for you. And I've bought myself something.' She stood up to see him to the door, kissed him goodbye. 'Try and keep them off my back, if you can. I need some space.'

Her father might have tried but he didn't succeed, though at least he kept his promise not to tell the others the real reason. Her mother rang Alix at work the next day and said angrily, 'Alix, this has gone far enough. Punishing Rhys is one thing, but to go as far as renting your own flat is ridiculous. You have to remember that Rhys has a very responsible job and he's used to putting it first.'

'Yes, Ma, no one knows that better than I do,' Alix said sardonically.

'If you go on this way you might lose him. Do you want that?'

'I'm sorry, I have to go. Todd wants me in his office. Goodbye.'

She put the receiver down on her mother's indignant voice and just hoped she wouldn't turn up at the flat. But the next person to phone was Rhys's father, wanting to take her out to lunch. Alix made an excuse and began to feel hunted, especially when his mother also phoned. She wasn't as angry as her own mother had been, or if she was she didn't let it show. She was most apologetic on Rhys's behalf, saying that it had all been his fault et cetera, et cetera. But in the end all she wanted to do was to persuade Alix to go back to him. 'He's missing you dreadfully, Alix, and is so unhappy. He loves you very much, you know.'

'No. No, I don't know,' Alix said in a strangled voice and slammed down the phone.

Todd was leaving early the following morning to go to Canada for a few days, but hadn't said anything about taking Alix with him. But he often didn't if it was for just a short time. There were letters to be finished before he went, documents he wanted to sign, so Alix was kept working late and it was almost seven before she left. The lift whispered down to the ground floor and she stepped out into the foyer. Rhys was waiting, sitting with his legs stretched out in front of him and casually crossed as he read the evening paper.

Alix said goodnight to the doorman and went to walk past him, but knew she wouldn't be allowed to get away with it. Getting quickly to his feet he dropped the paper and came to open the door for her, then caught her elbow as she went to turn away. 'Let's go out to dinner somewhere.'

'I don't want to go anywhere with you.'

'You have to eat,' he pointed out.

'Not with you I don't. There's only one thing I want from you.'

Rhys's face tightened. 'Yes, a divorce. So you keep telling me.'

'Sorry, two things. That, and for you to get your parents off my back!'

He frowned. 'Have they been getting at you, too?'

'What do you think? They want me to go trotting back to you like a good little girl, having made my point. Only they don't know that the point is that you don't love me; and that's already been proved—by you!'

'That isn't true.'

She gave an incredulous gasp. 'Are you trying to tell me that you were in love with me when you asked me to marry you?'

Alix asked the question indignantly, already knowing the answer, and wasn't surprised when Rhys's eyes drew into a frown. Some people went by, looking at them curiously, and he used it as an excuse to say shortly, 'This is hardly the place to talk about it.' Raising his arm, he waved to a cruising taxi and pushed her into it, ignoring her protests. 'Wheeler's,' he said to the driver.

'I've already said I don't want to have dinner with you,' Alix said angrily.

'Running away and hiding isn't going to solve this.'

'There's nothing to solve—and going in to work for the last two days is hardly hiding away.'

'It's possible to hide in a crowd,' Rhys pointed out.

She had no answer to that and turned away to look out of the window. Rhys, too, was silent, but she was aware that he was watching her, studying her almost, as though he'd never really looked at her before. But he didn't say anything until they reached the famous fish restaurant and he put a compelling hand under her elbow when she held back. 'If you want me to treat you like an adult, then stop behaving like a sulky child,' he said shortly.

Alix glared at him, but let him lead her inside, to a table in a sheltered corner booth where they couldn't be overheard.

When the waiter came with the menus Rhys ordered aperitifs without consulting her. But he did say, 'What would you like to eat?'

She shrugged. 'I'm not hungry.'

'You should be—you're looking thin,' Rhys remarked.

'Well, I'm not.'

'Is this martyr act supposed to make me feel even sorrier, Alix?'

She turned to face him, her dark-shadowed eyes bitter. 'It isn't an act, and I don't care how you feel.'

His mouth tightened, and for a moment Alix thought she saw angry despair in his eyes. But that couldn't be right. She turned away again.

The drinks came, and Rhys ordered for them both, telling the waiter to bring a bottle of wine with the meal. Picking up his glass, Rhys said, 'Where did you disappear to, urchin?'

'Don't call me that,' she said tonelessly.

Rhys's fingers tightened on the glass. 'Sorry. Well, where did you go?'

'Does it matter?'

'Everything you do matters to me,' he answered evenly.

That made her laugh; a bitter mirthless sound. 'Since when?' she said jeeringly.

'Always. Haven't I always looked after you, helped you whenever I could? Next to my family, you've always been the closest person in the world to me. You know that.'

'Are you trying to make me feel guilty—saying I ought to be grateful?'

'No, of course not. I just want you to remember that we go back a long way, Alix. That we've always been close.'

She shook her head. 'No, we were never close. I thought we were, but what I've found out about you has made me realise that I never really knew you at all.' She shrugged. 'It isn't your fault. I always hero-worshipped you. I thought that you were—perfect, I suppose. That's why I wouldn't believe Lynette when she told me the truth.'

'She told you that I was marrying you to get Todd's job, right?'

'Yes, of course.'

Rhys said forcefully, 'Do you really think that Todd would allow his father's old-fashioned ideas to stop him from appointing the man he wanted for the job? Of course he wouldn't. OK, he does lip service to the old man's ideals, but Todd is a realist; he doesn't allow it to interfere with his running of the company. I would have been appointed as his successor in England whether I was married or not. Todd told you that himself.'

'He told you I'd asked him?'

'Yes, of course. He apologised to me in case Lynette had upset you. But he also said that he'd reassured you and that you'd been perfectly happy about it. And I think you were happy until the emergency came up in Lithuania and I had to go away. Then your resentment—your justified resentment—brought it into your mind again, and you magnified the whole thing out of proportion.'

'Is that what you think?' she said shortly.

'Yes.' Rhys's voice was steady and his eyes intent on her face. 'That's what I think.'

'I don't believe you,' she said flatly. 'I phoned old Mr Weston's assistant in Canada and she told me it was company policy only to give preferment to married men.' She held up a hand as Rhys went to protest. 'I know you're going to say that Todd would have ignored it, but she also told me that Mr Weston was having second thoughts about you until you got engaged.'

There was anger in Rhys's voice as he said, 'I can't help what she told you, but *I'm* telling you that it isn't so. Would you take the word of a stranger rather than mine?'

'Yes,' Alix said without hesitation, 'I would.' Rhys gritted his teeth. '*She* has no reason to lie to me,' Alix added.

'And why do you think I need to lie to you?'

She smiled faintly at that. 'You still need a wife.'

Reaching out, Rhys put his hand under her chin, turned her head and made her look at him. 'I want *you*. The girl I married, the girl I *chose* to marry. Not for any job; that was incidental. I would have married you anyway.'

'How gratifying,' Alix said sarcastically, pushing his hand away. 'I wonder why it is I don't believe you.'

'I've never lied to you, urchin,' Rhys said, with such sincerity in his voice that a great wave of hatred rose in her at his hypocrisy.

Turning to look at him, the hatred blazing in her eyes, she said, 'Haven't you? Is that why you never answered my question before—so that you didn't have to lie to me? Not that you have to,' she added contemptuously, 'I already know the answer.'

'The question being whether I was in love with you when I asked you to marry me, I take it?' Rhys said grimly. Alix was surprised, she'd thought he'd duck it, and even more surprised when he shook his head and said, 'No, not the way you mean. I cared about you a great deal—I always have—but I wasn't in love with you.'

She stared at him, taken aback by his honesty, then blinked and looked away, feeling dead inside. She wouldn't have believed him if he'd said he was in love with her—but he hadn't even cared enough to damn well lie!

The waiter came with the food, another with the wine. For a few minutes it was all bustle around her, but Alix sat dumbly through it, not even noticing when they'd gone. Her heart felt as if it had had a bad shock, and she realised that against all the odds she had subconsciously still been hoping that Rhys loved her. Well, now that last hope was gone and there was nothing left. Just this cold, heavy feeling of despair in her heart.

'Here.'

Rhys was holding out a glass of wine to her. Alix dug her nails into her palm until it hurt, then reached out to take the glass, forcing her hand not to shake. 'Thanks,' she managed in a voice that sounded distinctly odd.

'Eat your food.'

She glanced down, saw that he had ordered soup for her. Because it was something to do, something she could concentrate on, she picked up her spoon and began to eat.

When she'd finished, Rhys said, 'So aren't you going to ask me why I proposed to you?'

'No. I already know.'

'And, to a large extent, you're right,' Rhys admitted, bringing her eyes round to his face again. 'I began to think it was about time I got married—not for the job, but because I was ready to settle down, I suppose. To have those grandchildren my parents were always on about.' He paused, then said, 'I had never really fallen in love—oh, there had been a few adolescent infatuations, certainly—but not the real kind of love that you read about; that knocks you sideways and lasts forever. I hadn't been lucky enough to find that.' Alix lowered her eyes, couldn't look at him. But Rhys went on steadily, 'So when I thought of marriage, I thought of you. The girl next door. A girl who said she was in love with me, and who had so many qualities that I found—lovable.'

'Yes, like being malleable, and so besotted that you thought you could put me in a cupboard whenever you didn't feel like being married and take me out again when you got back from living your own life,' Alix interjected acidly.

'Yes, perhaps,' Rhys acknowledged. 'But there was also your innocence and your love of life, your courage and your steadfastness.'

'Oh, please,' Alix said on a mock embarrassed note. 'Spare my blushes.'

Rhys's mouth tightened, but he stayed silent as the waiter came up again, cleared the plates and served the next course. He filled their glasses again.

Alix looked down at her plate; it was Dover sole and looked absolutely delicious. She thought that if she tried to eat even a mouthful she would be ill. Sitting back she said, 'So you decided I would be suitable and you proposed to me just in time to quiet old Mr Weston's worries. *Do* go on.'

Rhys took a swallow of wine. 'I thought you too young to be married. I wanted to give ourselves time to get to know one another better,' Rhys told her. 'As adults. As potential lovers.'

'But, not being in love with me, you couldn't bring yourself to go to bed with me. Most understandable,' Alix said, inflicting self-torture. 'I wonder you didn't marry Donna Temple; then you wouldn't have had any trouble.'

'Donna isn't the type of girl one marries.'

Her lip curling contemptuously, Alix said, 'What a male chauvinist remark. What makes men so different? I bet you've slept with as many partners as she has. You certainly have that reputation.'

Rhys looked momentarily startled. 'Do I? It isn't true.' He shook his head as if putting Donna and his past out of his mind. 'You were special, Alix. Maybe that was something I told myself, but it's what I felt. I wanted everything to be right for you, for a white wedding to have the meaning it should have. Not just be an ancient rite gone through for form's sake to legalise a relationship that had been going on for months. You were the girl I'd been protecting for the last eighteen years, and I suppose I couldn't break the habit.' He noticed she hadn't even picked up her knife and fork and said, 'Eat your food.'

'No.'

He glanced at her set face and didn't push it, went on, 'I don't know why I kept putting off the wedding. Perhaps because I was subconsciously hoping that the love of my life might still come along; that the all-consuming love I'd always heard so much about would hit me, too.'

'But it didn't, so you married good old stand-by Alix,' she said in a dead voice.

'No, it didn't—*not then*,' Rhys stressed.

Her eyes widened as the implication sank in. Alix felt that she'd taken a great many blows tonight but this was, surely, to be the most devastating. Gripping her hands tightly together under the table, she somehow turned to look at him. For a minute her voice didn't seem to work, but then she said, 'Do you—do you mean that you've fallen in love with someone after all?'

'Yes,' he said softly, his eyes holding hers. 'With *you*. On the night you walked out on me. Seeing you then, so proud and defiant, it hit me like a kick in the stomach—I'd fallen in love with my own wife!'

She stared at him, saw the look of confident expectation in his eyes. More angry than she'd ever felt in her life, Alix stood up, picked up her glass of wine and threw it in his face. 'You liar!' she yelled at him. 'You dirty, lying swine!' With a violent shove she pushed the table out of the way and rushed out of the restaurant.

'Alix, can you come in here, please?' Todd's voice echoed over the intercom and she immediately took up her notepad and went into his office.

He was alone, sitting in the big leather swivel chair, drumming his fingers on the desk. It was Monday of the following week. Todd had got back from Canada on the Friday, so Alix guessed that he would have a lot of work for her. She seemed to do most of his work now, Brenda taking a back seat and content to do so. Usually he clipped out instructions, letters, memos, getting through the pile of papers on his desk fast, but this morning he seemed to be abstracted, and it was several minutes before his fingers became still and he raised his head to look at her.

'Alix, I have something to tell you. Lynette and I are splitting up, getting a divorce. She's met someone else, an Englishman, and wants to marry him, stay in England.'

'Oh, I'm so sorry,' Alix sympathised.

'Sorry—but not surprised,' Todd remarked, looking at her face.

Alix shook her head. 'No, there have been—rumours.'

Todd rubbed a hand across his face. 'I guessed as much.' He paused, then said heavily, 'You know, Alix, the failure of a marriage, breaking up with someone you love—that's the hardest thing a person can ever go through.'

Quickly she looked down at the notepad in her hands. 'Yes, I suppose it must be,' she answered, trying to keep her voice level.

Todd sighed, lost in his own thoughts for a minute, then said, 'I've only been staying on in England in the hope of getting Lynette to change her mind, getting her to come back to me, but as there's no longer any hope of that there's nothing to keep me here.'

'Your sons?' Alix ventured.

'We've come to an agreement about them. They're to go to school here and spend their holidays in Canada until they are old enough to choose for themselves. Lynette may have more children; she's still young enough. I really don't know what the hell's going to happen.' He fell into a moment of despondency, then shook himself and said more briskly, 'So, I'm going to Canada and Rhys will, of course, be taking over from me here.'

'When will you be leaving?'

'Within the next few weeks. I have to close up the house, that kind of thing.'

'Then I'll make sure that I'm ready to leave at the same time.'

Todd's bushy eyebrows drew into a frown. 'That isn't what I meant.'

She gave a tight smile. 'I'm your PA; of course I'm coming with you.'

'I appreciate it, Alix, but your place is here with Rhys.'

'He has his own secretary.'

'Yeah, but you're his wife and he'll want you at home here in London.'

Alix hesitated, looking down at her pad again, then licked lips gone dry and said, 'Todd, there's something I have to tell you, too. You see——'

But he said, 'First, maybe I should tell you that Rhys decided at the last minute to come to Canada with me last week.'

Her head came up at that and Alix said, 'Oh, I see,' on a note of understanding. She'd wondered why Rhys hadn't followed her to her flat that night, hadn't been waiting for her when she'd finished work since. She'd hoped that he'd given up on her and been glad of it, told herself firmly that she was glad. Now she said angrily, 'And just what did he say?'

'We talked on the plane,' Todd admitted. 'Rhys said that you and he were having a few problems settling down.'

'Really?' Alix said, at her most frigid.

'Now don't go all English on me. I'm very fond of both of you and I don't want to see you unhappy.'

'I'm not unhappy.'

He gave a snort of disbelief at that one. 'Have you looked at yourself in the mirror lately? For a new bride just back from her honeymoon—well, you just don't look the part!'

'Is that why you've decided to go back to Canada now?' she demanded. 'Did Rhys persuade you to?' Then answered her own question by exclaiming, 'I might have known! That's just typical of him.'

'I don't think you're being fair, Alix. I——'

'Why the hell should I be fair?' she interrupted fiercely. 'He's used me again—to gain your sympathy. And taken advantage of your splitting up with Lynette to persuade you to go to Canada immediately, just so he can take over your job!'

'The job was already promised to him months ago,' Todd pointed out. He frowned at her. 'What the hell's gotten into you, Alix? Anyone would think you hated the guy!'

'Anyone might be right.' She bit her inner lip, then tried to say steadily, 'Todd, I want to go to Canada with you. You know Brenda won't go. And you've licked me into shape by now; what's the point of training someone new?'

He shook his head decisively. 'No. I'm not going to be responsible for breaking up someone else's marriage. I know what it's like.'

'You wouldn't be. Our—our marriage never really got started. I'm seeing a lawyer; I'm getting a divorce.' That was an exaggeration because she hadn't brought herself to see a solicitor yet, but it sounded irrevocable.

Todd stared at her. 'You've done that?' His voice grew angry. 'You've only been married for a month or so; what the hell kind of chance have you given Rhys? Does he know about this?'

'Not yet,' she admitted.

Getting to his feet angrily, Todd said, 'Then I suggest you both get together and sort this out before you do something stupid.' He rounded on her. 'Is all this because Lynette shot her mouth off? Because you think that Rhys needed to be married? Because if it is, I can tell you here and now, Alix, that it wasn't true. I'll choose whoever I damn well want for this job: married or single, male or female. Do you understand?'

'It isn't because of that,' Alix said shortly. 'It's—it's much more basic than that.' She hesitated, then said pleadingly, 'Please take me with you to Canada, Todd.

Nothing on earth will get Rhys and me together again. I'm quite certain of that. And to go to Canada, to get right away from Rhys and our parents, would be exactly what I need. Please, Todd.'

He stood looking down at her for a moment, but she could see from the anger in his face that he wasn't going to do as she asked. 'No. You'll stay here where you belong.'

'Then I'll resign,' she threatened.

'OK, go ahead. But you signed a contract to give three months' notice—and I'm going to hold you to that.'

She looked at him coldly. 'What are you trying to do?'

'I don't know. But Rhys is my friend, and I'm sure as hell not going to give him reason to say that I helped to break up his marriage.'

'I told you; it's already over! I don't——'

But Todd rounded on her angrily. 'Get out of here, Alix, before I damn well lose my temper.'

He wasn't the only person who was angry with her. Her mother had shown up at the flat last week and had been more impatient than Alix had ever known her. Then Rhys's parents had come to the office 'to take them out to lunch' as they'd put it, and she'd had to go with them alone, to tell them she didn't know where Rhys was. They hadn't been openly angry with her, had tried to be so understanding that she came close to tears, but they had left in a mood of silent resentment at her obstinacy. But all this parental pressure only served to make Alix even more determined; she had been a dutiful daughter all her life, but now she had to make her own decisions, somehow get out of this mess and start again.

It was a relief when Todd reminded her that they were due to fly to Alaska at the weekend. 'The company jet won't be available, so we'll take scheduled flights to

Juneau. I'll be there for a couple of days, and then the jet will pick us up and take us to the site. Oh, and my elder boy will be coming with us for the trip. I'm hoping I'll be able to get a couple of days off to take him fishing.'

Alix duly booked the seats, packed her bag, and was happy to get away. Rhys, too, had flown off on some new project, so she was saved having to decide whether or not to tell him where she was going, but he probably knew anyway. Todd's son, Martin, was an eleven-year-old duplicate of what his father must have been like at that age: a little short and stocky, but with a big grin and a happy, extrovert manner; into all the latest video games and gadgets.

Their two days at Juneau were busy ones, with Martin amusing himself going round the town, while Todd attended several meetings with the local government, making contacts, getting information, boosting the company image. Alix was with him most of the time, and did a lot of work in her hotel room at night, leaving Todd free to be with Martin. They had Wednesday morning free then drove out to the airport in the afternoon to pick up the company jet, which had flown up from Canada to meet them. They were to fly north to the Yukon river, almost as far as the Arctic Circle, to investigate the possibilities of building a hydro-electric plant that would benefit both Canada and Alaska.

The very word Alaska had made Alix expect it to be cold, but it was a beautifully warm summer day. The pilot greeted them with a broad smile, Martin was happy and excited, even Todd seemed more relaxed as they boarded the plane. Todd politely stood back to let Alix go on board first, but came up close behind her. So she had nowhere to go as Rhys got to his feet and said, 'Hello, Alix. Come and sit here.'

CHAPTER EIGHT

ALIX instinctively backed away when she saw Rhys, but Todd's bulk propelled her forward and she somehow found herself in the window seat with Rhys beside her.

She went to express her anger at this plan they'd obviously hatched up between them, but Martin came on board and smiled at Rhys. 'Hello, Mr Stirling. I didn't know you were coming with us.'

'A last-minute arrangement,' Rhys said smoothly. 'How are you, Martin?'

'Fine. Dad's going to take me fishing.' He dropped his bulging canvas travel-bag on one of the seats and sat in the one across the aisle from Rhys.

'Ever been fishing before?' Rhys asked.

'Oh, yes.'

Martin began to tell him of his lifetime's fishing experience and Alix had to be content with a furious glance at Todd before he went to sit beside the pilot. But Todd just grinned and said, 'Don't forget to do your seatbelts up, folks.'

They took off smoothly, but Rhys gave his attention to Martin until the subject of fishing was exhausted and the boy opened his bag to take out one of his pocket games and play with it.

Rhys turned to Alix and she gave him an antagonistic glare, but couldn't help noticing that there was a drawn look about his eyes and mouth, as if he hadn't been

sleeping very well. So that makes two of us, she thought
resentfully. Deliberately she turned her head to look out
of the window at the landscape of mountains, forests
and lakes far below, but Rhys reached across and picked
up her left hand.

'This looks very bare. What excuse have you given for
not wearing the rings?'

'Does it matter?' she said curtly and pulled her hand
free.

Rhys didn't try to stop her, which rather surprised Alix,
but said mildly, 'Suppose I'm asked why you're not
wearing them; it would look rather strange if I invented
an entirely different excuse.'

Alix saw the sense in that, so said reluctantly, 'I said
that they'd gone to be altered.'

He nodded. 'I'll remember. But why bother to make
up a reason? Why didn't you just tell everyone the truth?'

A flush of colour came into Alix's cheeks. 'It's our
business, not anyone else's.'

'True—and yet you've been to see a solicitor.'

Alix shot a venomous glance at Todd's back which
she could see through the open door of the cockpit. 'You
need a legal separation so that you can get a divorce in
two years,' she pointed out stiffly.

'Ah, yes. So when did this legal separation start? I
haven't been notified about it.'

'It hasn't yet,' Alix mumbled.

'Sorry, I didn't hear you.'

Angry eyes came up to meet his. 'I said it hasn't—
yet.'

Rhys's mouth twisted into a small smile. 'You know,
urchin, you really shouldn't try lying to me. I can always

tell when you do; always have been able to. You haven't been to a solicitor, have you?'

She flushed a little and shook her head, thinking that it was true; she could get away with lying to other people but never with Rhys, he'd always seen through her—or maybe it was because she'd loved him so much that she'd never really *wanted* to lie to him. 'No, but I intend to,' she said firmly. 'I just haven't—got around to it yet.'

'I see.' Changing tactics, he said, 'I heard my parents came to see you. I'm sorry if they upset you, but it's rather difficult for them, you see, because they can't understand why we don't settle this.'

'It is settled as far as I'm concerned.'

'Is it?' Rhys's eyes studied her face, so dark and intense that she had to look away. 'I rather hoped we could discuss it while we're in Alaska.'

That made her gulp inwardly; she hadn't thought that he might stay on with them, hadn't thought further than this plane trip. 'There's nothing to discuss,' she said hurriedly. 'You're wasting your time. It's over.'

Her voice had risen and Martin glanced across at them. Rhys gave her a warning frown, then stood up. 'I'll see if the others want a drink.' He went to the cockpit, was there a few minutes, came back and took a couple of cans from the fridge. 'Perhaps you'd like to take these, Martin?' he suggested.

Shoving his game in his pocket, Martin went willingly enough. They heard Todd greet him and say, 'Hey, son, how about a flying lesson?' He gave up his seat to Martin and deliberately closed the cockpit door, leaving them alone.

'I suppose you arranged that, too?' Alix said bitterly.

'I'll go to whatever lengths I have to to get you to talk to me,' Rhys admitted. Coming back to sit beside her, he said, 'I really feel we need some time together to——'

Alix, who had begun to feel hunted again, broke in with a forceful, 'No! I don't want to be near you. If you insist on staying I shall get on the first plane out of there.'

'Coward!' Rhys said scathingly.

That brought her up short. Alix thought she'd been pretty brave about this whole thing most of the time. 'I'm—I'm not.'

'Of course you are. You ran away from our honeymoon and you've been running ever since. And not only physically but mentally, too. Every time I've tried to talk to you you've shut me out, refusing to even listen.'

'I don't see much point in listening to your lies,' she retaliated.

Rhys took hold of her arm, gripped it tight. 'I have *never* lied to you,' he said vehemently, his eyes holding hers, his whole face behind his words.

His forcefulness shook her. 'You—you admitted you never loved me,' she faltered.

'And I told you the truth. But I think it was more a case of being in love with you for so long that I hadn't seen it for what it was. It was only when you threatened to walk out on me that I realised just how much you meant to me. And when you went away and I couldn't find you I was completely devastated. It was only then that I knew how empty my life would have been without you—would always be if I didn't get you back.' His eyes burned into hers. 'I wasn't head over heels in love with you before, Alix, but I am now. Passionately. Madly in love. And I'll spend my whole life convincing you of that, if I have to.'

She stared at him, never having seen him like this before. Rhys wasn't the type of man to show his feelings so openly; that he could do so now had her halfway believing him. A small flicker of emotion entered her heart, an emotion that was suppressed before it could be defined, and Alix said bleakly, 'The job. How can I believe you?'

Impatiently, Rhys took her hand and said, 'Haven't you been told enough times that the job is immaterial? And if it had mattered, if I had married you for that, wouldn't I have lied and told you that I'd always loved you? Would I have taken the risk of telling you the truth?'

Alix looked at him, felt a desperate need to believe him, but she had gone through so much pain and misery these last few weeks. Her face set, she said, 'What does it matter anyway? You may be telling the truth; perhaps my standing up to you did make you fall in love with me. The lure of the unobtainable,' she said on a caustic note. 'But it's too late. Because I don't love *you* any more, Rhys.' She gave a travesty of a smile. 'How ironic. That you should fall for me while I fall out of love with you.'

'I don't believe that,' Rhys said with absolute certainty in his voice.

'I can't help what you believe,' she said tiredly. 'It happens to be true.'

Still holding her hand, he said, 'OK, maybe you think it is. But I'm sure that it's just a defence you've created in your mind to help you. You've loved me for a long time, Alix; you couldn't change so completely.'

'Well, I have.'

Rhys looked at her intently, then gave a slow smile, a promise in the depths of his eyes. 'Then I'll just have to make you fall in love with me again, won't I?'

Again that flutter in her heart. 'You'd be wasting your time.'

'Somehow I don't think so. But what better way to spend my time—telling my wife how much I love her.'

'I'm—I'm not your wife any longer,' Alix said faintly.

Raising her hand to his lips, he kissed it, his eyes holding hers. 'Oh, but you are, my sweet.' His grip tightened and there was purpose in his face as he said, 'And you always will be. Because you're mine, Alix, and I'll *never* let you go.' Reaching into his pocket, he took out her rings and held her hand in a firm grip as he put them on to her finger.

Alix remembered the last time he had put the rings on her finger and said, in defiance of her stupid heart, 'Wearing those won't make me feel any different.'

'No, but you're going to need them. You see, I've booked a cabin in the mountains for us so that we can be together. And I've booked it for Mr and Mrs Stirling.'

This time her heart gave a great lurch, and her body filled with nervous dread, because she knew what he meant by 'being together'. He would make love to her again and she would be lost, unable to fight the closeness, the fulfilment that her body craved. She opened her mouth to protest, but whatever she might have said was lost, because there came a sudden uproar of voices from the cockpit and Martin came running out, his face chalk-white.

'Martin! What is it?'

'It wasn't my fault,' he burst out. 'I didn't know there was a magnet in the game. I didn't know we'd get lost!'

They stared at him, then Rhys got quickly to his feet. 'Of course you didn't. Here, come and sit with Alix while I go and see if I can help.'

Alix reached out for the boy but raised a dismayed face to Rhys. He gave her a reassuring smile, then went forward, shutting the door behind him. It seemed ages before he came back. Again he smiled, but Alix could see the strain around his mouth.

'Unfortunately Martin's game played havoc with the navigational aids, but we're back on course again now. But the pilot has decided that when we pick up a radio signal from another airfield we'll drop in there to have the instruments checked, just to be on the safe side. It means we'll be a bit late getting to our destination, that's all.'

For when read if, Alix realised with horror. But she said nothing, not wanting to frighten the boy. Looking out of the window, she saw that they were flying over what appeared to be endless miles of forest, the trees very thick with very few patches of open ground. And the sun was sinking now; soon it would be dark. Turning back, she smiled and said, 'I'm hungry. Is there anything to eat?'

'I bought some chocolate bars in Juneau,' Martin said, eager to make up for his mistake. 'I brought them to take on the fishing trip.'

'Great! Let's have a look what you've got.'

They shared a bar of chocolate and then played a card game, trying to dispel the tension. Without warning the cockpit door was pushed open and Todd called out for Rhys. It was dark now, the lights on in the cabin. Martin's hand reached out and gripped Alix's. She looked at him and put her arm around him, seeing him close to tears. 'It's all my fault,' he said.

'Rubbish! The pilot should have checked what you had with you.'

When he came back she could see in Rhys's face that it was bad, even though he tried to hide it. He said, 'It seems we might have a bumpy landing. We've to get ourselves ready. Come on, Martin, you first.'

Alix expected Rhys to just strap the boy in his seat, but first he wrapped him in blankets and a sleeping bag that the pilot kept on board. She knew then that they were going to crash.

'Now you, urchin.'

Rhys wrapped her in the rest of the blankets, cushioned her with pillows. 'No, take some for yourself and the others,' she protested.

'Don't you ever do as you're told?' he complained. 'I can see I'm going to go on having trouble with you for the rest of my life.'

Immediately, they both realised what he'd said. Rhys looked rueful, but he leaned forward and kissed her, deeply, lingeringly as a man did when he knew it might be for the last time. 'My love,' he whispered. 'Oh, God, Alix, I love you so much!'

The engine coughed and the plane lurched. Rhys grabbed the arm rest but didn't attempt to sit down. Alix gave a terrified look out of the window. Then shouted,

'Look! There are lights. Over to the left. Oh, they're hidden now.'

'I'll go and tell them. They may not have seen.'

Rhys ran forward and immediately the plane swung to port. But it was going down now, gliding, the engine silent as the last of the fuel was used up. Alix's eyes searched frantically for the lights but she couldn't see them again. Oh, God, what if she'd made a mistake? What if it was only the moon shining on water?

The plane fell lower. Rhys came running back up the slope of the floor, but instead of strapping himself into a seat he flung himself on top of her, covering her body with his own. 'No! You mustn't. Rhys, please.'

But he clung on, gripping the back of the seat. Dimly she was aware that Todd was in the cabin, was shielding Martin in the same way. There was a terrible rushing, cracking noise, the plane seemed to bounce along the tops of the trees, their branches tearing at the fuselage like demons trying to get in. The lights went out, things were flying about the cabin, lethal, dangerous. There was the most ghastly groan from the battered plane and then a rush of cold air as the right wing was torn off. Someone gave a cry of pain and she felt Rhys's body jerk. Her arms went round him and Alix clung to him, trying to be his seatbelt as the terrible noises seemed to go on for ever. They seemed suddenly to drop into a chasm of emptiness, there was one last, horrific crunch as the whole plane seemed to fall apart, and then just silence—a noiselessness that seemed somehow far worse than everything that had gone before.

The gasping moan of a man in pain broke the quiet.

'Rhys?' Alix's terrified anxiety for Rhys broke through her own shock and terror at the plane crash. He didn't answer and she realised that his body was heavy across hers. '*Rhys!*' She cried out his name in agony, shook him violently, convinced that he was dead. He stirred, mumbled something, and Alix knew with life-giving relief that he wasn't dead, and that it wasn't him who was moaning in pain.

He came to quickly, and seemed to grasp immediately what had happened 'We must get out,' he said hoarsely.

'Somebody's hurt; I can hear him.'

The plane was lying at an angle, leaning on its right hand side, where the wing had been. Rhys pushed himself upright, groped his way through torn seats and debris to the door and kicked it open. Mechanically Alix undid her seat belt and got to her feet, but found that all the strength seemed to have gone out of her legs. Rhys caught her before she fell and half carried her to the door.

'Martin?' she exclaimed. 'Todd?'

'I'll take care of them. Come on.' Taking her to the door, Rhys lowered her the few feet to the ground. 'Get away from the plane,' he ordered brusquely. 'Go on, my darling girl, get right away.'

'Oh, Rhys!' She gave a low moan of terror, knowing he was afraid the plane would catch fire, but she obeyed him, stumbling away from the plane into the night, blundering into bushes, her eyes unaccustomed to the darkness. She came to a tree, sank down behind its great trunk, unable to go any further, but then twisted round to look towards the plane.

She could see it now, its white-painted fuselage caught in a shaft of moonlight. From here it still looked remarkably intact, just drunk. Oh, God, please don't let it blow up, she prayed. Don't let it catch fire. She saw Rhys come to the door again, helping someone down through it, a large figure that must be Todd. He stood on the ground below, holding on to the door frame, almost collapsing. Then Rhys came holding Martin in his arms, lowering him for Todd to take. Instantly Alix was up and running towards them, knowing that Todd couldn't manage the boy alone.

'Here, let me,' she called out.

'Alix!' Rhys's voice was tense with fear for her.

'I must help. What about the pilot?'

'He's alive. I'm going to him now.'

Somehow, between them, Todd and Alix managed to carry Martin out of danger. Todd was limping badly and his left arm hung uselessly at his side. When they reached the tree and put Martin down, he grunted out, 'You— look after him. I'll go back—help Rhys.'

'No, you can't! You're hurt. I'll go.'

Todd tried to protest but she was already gone, able to see better now and avoid the bushes. Rhys was still inside the plane. Hoisting herself up, Alix went in to find him. He was in what was left of the cockpit, trying to free the pilot's trapped legs. When he saw her, he could only shake his head and say, 'Oh, Alix.'

She smiled. 'That's what I usually say to you.'

His eyes widened, settled on her face for an incredulous moment, but then he became practical again and said, 'Can you pull his leg free if I can lever this piece of metal away?'

'Of course.'

The poor man cried out in pain when she touched him, but somehow they pulled him free.

'He's bleeding badly,' she said in distress, feeling the blood on her hands.

'The first-aid kit; see if you can find it. It should be here in the cockpit somewhere.'

Alix groped around, cut her hand on a piece of metal, but found the box and, oh, thank God, there was a torch inside it. Rhys worked quickly and efficiently, stopping the bleeding, putting on a thick dressing, then splinting up his broken legs.

'All right, let's try and get him out. I'll take his head. Try and be as careful as you can with his legs.'

They had trouble getting him out of the door, but somehow they managed it and carried him over to the others. Martin had come round and his father was holding him while he was being sick. Rhys put the pilot down and straightened up. 'I'll go back and get the first-aid kit.'

'No, Rhys, please,' Alix said in distress.

He put a reassuring hand on her shoulder. 'If the plane was going to go up it would have gone by now. I'll be back in just a few minutes.'

He was longer than that, and when he returned he was laden with blankets, cushions, drinks, Martin's bag, as well as the first-aid box. They were busy, then, the two of them, working as a team to make the pilot more comfortable, putting Todd's arm in a splint and a sling, taking a look at his leg and putting a dressing on it, examining Martin and finding that he was shaking with shock but otherwise seemed to be unhurt. They gave Martin a drink and some chocolate, wrapping everyone in blankets, trying to keep them warm, lit a fire of twigs and leaves.

Only then, when there was nothing else she could do did Alix relax and find that she was completely exhausted. She sank to the ground, her legs like jelly, and found that she was suddenly shaking uncontrollably. Rhys had gone back to the plane and came back with a lot more things, including some water to heat over the fire in the drink cans to make coffee. Alix was sitting in the shadows and it was a few minutes before he came over to her. He put his arm round her, felt the convulsive tremors that ran through her and immediately drew her closer. 'It's all right,' he murmured. 'You're safe, little one.'

He comforted her like a child, stroking her hair, letting her feel the strength of his body. Alix wept a little, but presently became still, her head on his shoulder.

Rhys must have thought she'd fallen asleep, because he said softly to Todd, who was cradling his son in his good arm, 'Did you manage to get through to anyone on the radio?'

'We were sending out mayday signals the whole time, but we weren't sure of our position. But the lights Alix saw—the pilot thought he saw them up ahead just before we went down.'

'We should be able to find the place easily enough, then,' Rhys said confidently. 'I'll set off at first light.'

Alix sat up. 'Surely they'll be sending out search planes to look for us. They knew we were coming, didn't they? They might even be looking for us now.' Rhys threw another log on the fire, watched the sparks fly up—and then Alix understood. 'They don't know where we are, won't know where to look,' she said dully.

'No.' Rhys didn't try to hide it from her. 'So I'll have to go and get help.'

'If we kept the fire going,' Alix said on a desperate note, 'surely someone would see it, or see the smoke?'

'Very probably,' Rhys agreed. But he glanced towards the pilot and said, 'He needs medical attention quickly, Alix. I've given him some morphine to kill the pain but there isn't much left.'

She didn't argue any more but said firmly, 'Then you must get some sleep. Go on, I'll watch the fire.'

'OK, thanks.' He gave her a hug. 'Watch out for any passing grizzly bears.'

'They'd better watch out themselves,' she responded. 'We could do with their coats.'

Rhys woke a couple of times during the long hours of darkness; she could tell by the sudden tensing of his body, then he would relax again and after a while fall into another troubled sleep. The dawn seemed to break very slowly, just a lightening in the sky and then the shapes of the trees emerging slowly through the morning mist. The pilot had done wonderfully well; they seemed to have come down in the only patch of open ground for miles around, an area that must have been burned to the ground within the last couple of years, because there were only low bushes and saplings growing.

Alix set some more water on to heat and when it was boiling made some coffee, then woke Rhys. He turned over and it was only then that she saw the dried cut on his forehead.

'Rhys, your head.'

He put a hand up to it. 'Must have bumped it when the plane crashed.'

'It must have been that that knocked you out.'

He looked surprised. 'Was I out?'

'I thought you were dead,' Alix told him, inwardly shuddering at the fear she'd felt.

Perhaps it showed in her face, because Rhys drew her to him to kiss her. 'You didn't really think you'd get rid of me that easily, did you?' He drank the coffee, rose, and winced as he flexed his muscles.

Todd woke with a groan, rousing Martin. The boy was much better this morning but terribly white and subdued, still inwardly blaming himself for the crash. Rhys, however, made him look in his fishing gear for a knife, rescue the compass from the plane, and generally help him to get ready.

When he was, Alix stood up. 'I'm coming with you.'

Rhys kissed her but shook his head. 'No, my darling, you must stay here and look after the others. Be ready to attract the attention of a plane if one flies over.'

'But how can I possibly do that?'

'By setting fire to our plane,' he said steadily. 'Look, I've made it all ready for you.' He gave her Todd's lighter. 'All you have to do is set light to this petrol trail I've laid, then run like hell and get behind a tree. Do you think you can do that?'

'Yes, of course. But, Rhys, I can't let you go alone.'

'You must. Don't worry. Now, I must go. Walk with me a little way.' He said goodbye to the others then put his arm round Alix's waist as they walked out of sight among the trees.

'You'll mark a trail,' she said anxiously, fully prepared to follow him if he didn't come back.

'I promise.' Rhys kissed her then, kissed her with such passion that she reeled. He looked into her face for a long moment, then tore himself away and went striding off through the trees. When he was almost out of sight he looked back and waved.

Alix went slowly back, made the others as comfortable as she could, and sat down to watch—and worry.

She didn't have to set light to the plane. In the afternoon when the sun was hot overhead, she heard the unmistakable sound of a helicopter engine. Alix had been bathing the pilot's forehead, trying to calm what seemed to be a growing fever, and wondering if he ought to have another shot of morphine. Martin heard the helicopter at the same time and shouted excitedly. Together they ran out into the open, waving blankets, jumping up and down and yelling at the tops of their voices. The helicopter came low, hovered, and three men in flying suits and helmets jumped out.

For a moment Alix didn't recognise Rhys and she grabbed the first man. 'My husband! Have you seen my husband?'

He gestured behind him and then she saw the third man taking off his helmet. Rhys grinned at her. 'It was almost worth crashing to hear you call me that.'

Then she was in his arms and held very tightly as she sobbed out her relief.

It was night again, but the circumstances were so different now. The pilot was in hospital. He was going to be all right, the doctors had said, out of action for a few months until his legs mended, but then be as good as new. Martin and Todd, his arm set in plaster, were spending the night in a nursing home in the nearest town, waiting for Lynette to fly out to them. But father and son were comforting each other and keeping close. The doctors had wanted Alix and Rhys to stay in their care overnight, too, but both had refused. Instead they'd been driven to the log cabin that Rhys had rented, one very similar, he said, to the cabin that he had found earlier, and where he'd woken the surprised occupants only a couple of hours after he had set out for help.

Their battered suitcases had been rescued from the plane, the cabin had already been provisioned, and someone had lit the fire in the stone fireplace. They'd already eaten and bathed, back at the hospital. Now they drank a silent toast to each other and stood on the fur rug in the firelight, slowly undressing one another, the flickering shadows hiding the bruises, the dressing on Rhys's forehead where he would always have a scar. When they were naked he kissed her, going down on his knees in physical worship. Then he picked her up and carried her to the big, warm bed.

'Are you sure you're OK?' he murmured as he held her in his arms.

For answer Alix smiled and moved against him.

He groaned and was suddenly leaning over her, suddenly intense. 'Don't ever run away from me again,' he said forcefully. 'Swear you won't.'

Putting her hands on either side of his face, she gave him a teasing look. 'Oh, I might.' She felt him tense and said quickly, 'But only as far as the nearest bedroom— and only if you'll promise to catch me.'

Relaxing, he bit her ear lobe. 'Minx.' Then his eyes darkened and he pulled her to him, to make love to her with all the passion and urgency that she'd once glimpsed but never known, lovemaking that was a thousand light-years away from their wedding-night. And as he took her in a savage blaze of hunger, Alix knew that she'd found the love she'd always dreamt of at last.

Look out for Temptation's bright, new, stylish covers...

They're Terrifically Tempting!

We're sure you'll love the new raspberry-coloured Temptation books—our brand new look from December.

Temptation romances are still as passionate and fun-loving as ever and they're on sale now!

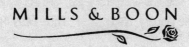

MILLS & BOON

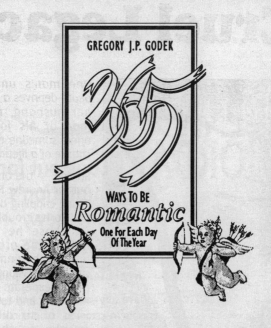

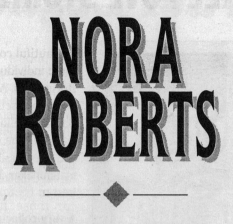

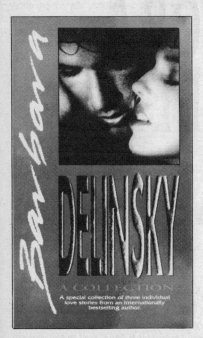

Next Month's Romances

Each month you can choose from a wide variety of romance with Mills & Boon. Below are the new titles to look out for next month, why not ask either Mills & Boon Reader Service or your Newsagent to reserve you a copy of the titles you want to buy – just tick the titles you would like and either post to Reader Service or take it to any Newsagent and ask them to order your books.

Please save me the following titles: Please tick   ✓

TRIAL BY MARRIAGE	*Lindsay Armstrong*	
ONE FATEFUL SUMMER	*Margaret Way*	
WAR OF LOVE	*Carole Mortimer*	
A SECRET INFATUATION	*Betty Neels*	
ANGELS DO HAVE WINGS	*Helen Brooks*	
MOONSHADOW MAN	*Jessica Hart*	
SWEET DESIRE	*Rosemary Badger*	
NO TIES	*Rosemary Gibson*	
A PHYSICAL AFFAIR	*Lynsey Stevens*	
TRIAL IN THE SUN	*Kay Thorpe*	
IT STARTED WITH A KISS	*Mary Lyons*	
A BURNING PASSION	*Cathy Williams*	
GAMES LOVERS PLAY	*Rosemary Carter*	
HOT NOVEMBER	*Ann Charlton*	
DANGEROUS DISCOVERY	*Laura Martin*	
THE UNEXPECTED LANDLORD	*Leigh Michaels*	

If you would like to order these books in addition to your regular subscription from Mills & Boon Reader Service please send £1.90 per title to: Mills & Boon Reader Service, Freepost, P.O. Box 236, Croydon, Surrey, CR9 9EL, quote your Subscriber No:................................. (if applicable) and complete the name and address details below. Alternatively, these books are available from many local Newsagents including W H Smith, J Menzies, Martins and other paperback stockists from 13 January 1995.

Name:...

Address:..

................................Post Code:..........................

To Retailer: If you would like to stock M&B books please contact your regular book/magazine wholesaler for details.

You may be mailed with offers from other reputable companies as a result of this application. If you would rather not take advantage of these opportunities please tick box.   ☐